A Hard Rain

D1557419

Dec 2018

A Hard Rain

Steven Lewis

For Annabel
with enduring affection
and boundless admiration.
Steve

Codhill Press
New Paltz, New York

Codhill Press books
are published for David Appelbaum

First Edition
Printed in the United States of America
Copyright © 2018 by Steven Lewis

ISBN 1-930337-99-X

All rights reserved. No part of this publication protected by this copyright notice may be reproduced or utilized in any form or by any means, electronic, mechanical, including photocopying, recording or by any informational storage and retrieval system, without written permission of the publisher.

Cover and interior design:
www.aliciafoxdesign.com

The wind howls like a hammer

—Bob Dylan,
"Love Minus Zero"

For Patti, into our eternity

It's knowing that this can't go on forever
Likely one of us will have to spend some days alone
Maybe we'll get forty years together
But one day I'll be gone
Or one day you'll be gone

—Jason Isbell,
"If We Were Vampires"

Acknowledgments

Abiding gratitude to the unfathomable universe for this life of grace I live—and about which I get to write.

My humblest thanks to brilliant writers Karen Dukess, David Masello, Annabel Monaghan, and Peter Steinfeld, who startled me with their gorgeous blessings.

Endless appreciation for Codhill's David Appelbaum and Susannah Appelbaum: "... the charming gardeners who make our souls blossom." (Marcel Proust)

Part 1: Spring 1972

Hatteras Island, NC

Chapter 1

A cool, sticky breeze lifts the white cotton curtains just beyond the foot of the bed, the ocean rushing in. Brenda, recently turned forty and still girlish in her satin nightshirt and long chestnut hair, stands at the mirror over the maple dresser. She brushes some sand off the glossy surface, opens a mostly-empty drawer, pulls out a white bra. She looks up and finds you watching her.

You are still in bed, hands behind your head, alternately watching your wife undress and glancing up at the popcorn ceiling and the dots of mildew around the vent.

She speaks into the smudged glass. "I don't want to go back, Peter."

You raise your eyebrows and let four or five breathless seconds pass, a weak smile flickering across your shadowy face. "I think I've heard that before," you say, turning toward the open window, the curtain fluttering again. "But we gotta go . . . things to do, places to go, people—"

"I mean it this time," she interrupts. "I really don't want to go back. I . . ." She presses her lips together and then opens them in a circle. The rumbling ocean behind the dunes seems to absorb the lull that follows, sucking it out to sea. And then returns it with another crash.

You turn and pull the frayed double-wedding-ring quilt up over your bare shoulder. It is the quilt Brenda had found in her grandmother's trunk—up in her blistering hot Avon attic—after the funeral. "We have to go home, babe. You know that."

"Well, I'm thinking that I actually don't know that. I think I used to accept it as true because you said it or someone else said it. But tell me why we have to go back? I mean, it's our life. We don't have to answer to anyone but ourselves."

You take a deep breath, mostly for effect, but it is one she knows so well there is no effect. And when you glance again in the smudged mirror around her shoulder. Brenda looks pale, distracted, eyes like the Ocracoke ponies, wilderness deep in the dark pupils, tears and terror along the smokey edges. The same sad yearning that first stirred you twenty years before in Chapel Hill. "I really thought we had this whole thing worked out last summer," you say.

"I can't do it." She shakes her head.

Now you push yourself up, bare back against the wicker headboard. "You know, Brenda, it's really hard, really hard that we have to go through this every time we leave here . . ." Your voice rises like a small search plane. "I mean, just listen to yourself for a minute. You make it sound like it's some kind of prison back home."

"It is."

"You're the one who once told me you never wanted to come back to this island—ever."

She shakes her head again. "That was a long time ago, Peter. A long, long time ago and everything's changed. I'm changed. You're changed. I know you know what I'm talking about."

Your voice is just above a whisper. "No, I don't."

"Don't you wonder what it would be like?" She drops the bra and lifts the loose nightshirt over her head, revealing a smooth sloping back, soft white hips, cotton panties. "Peter?"

Another deep breath: "Yeah, sure, you know I do. Y'know, it isn't nearly as bleak and pointless as you make it sound back home. Most of the world would sell their souls to live like us."

"And that's just what they'd have to do," she says.

"What about—"

"I'll quit. I quit," she answers your unasked question about her position at the real estate agency.

"And the kids? They have to go to school."

She frowns. "They have a school here. They'll go down to Buxton with the rest of the island kids. I did it. It won't be Rosslyn schools—thank God—but they'll survive." She smiles.

"Well, we have to go back. You know that. They have friends, school—I have a good job." You check the mirror and find her eyes. "You have a good job. And why am I telling you this? Why am I always pleading with you to come back to your own good home?"

"Because we're dying."

"Oh Jesus Christ, Brenda, we're alive and well." You slap the soft mattress with the flat of your hand. "Let's just pack, be sad, jump in the van, and go home. We'll come back down in August." You try to swallow the trembling in your throat. "Three months. It's not that long, babe."

"It's a lifetime," she says, picking up the bra, dangling it from a finger, dropping it again in the opened drawer, pushing the drawer shut, reaching now for a red hooded sweatshirt missing the string.

You push away the quilt and swivel out of the bed, reaching down to the cluttered suitcase for the bunched-up Levi's. A white T-shirt. "I just want to go home."

"We are home." She smiles a little slanted now, her voice cooing. She picks up the brush and runs it through her long, thick hair once, twice, three times, her voice now as cottony as the soft flesh on her hips. "I'm sorry, Peter, I really am. I know I should be going about this differently. But I just can't do that anymore. I know you don't see it, but I'm in danger. I'm afraid I'm gonna unravel. I feel like I'm going to disappear if I go back there. All I can think about when I'm in Rosslyn is this sand and this sky . . . and the wind, Peter, the wind. I'm so sorry." Tears dribble down her cheeks.

You walk around the bed, coming up behind her, your arms

around her waist, under her sweatshirt, nuzzling her ear. "I know, sweetheart, I know . . . let's not fight. When we get back to Rosslyn we'll have Sarah watch the boys—she's old enough now—and we'll go into DC for a long weekend—just you and me. And we can make love and talk about moving here seriously . . . maybe after Woody graduates from high school." You slide your cool hand up on her warm and heavy breast.

She leans back against you, her voice a whisper. "I don't think I can wait that long, Peter. I can't do it." She rolls her head at the touch of your lips. "I'm in trouble." And with that she pushes up her shoulder to get you to stop the nuzzling, but you've already stopped, your hands dropping down to her hips and then to your own.

She walks to the window, the wind blowing her hair. "You can open a small newspaper, like you've been talking about for years. Years, Peter. I used to draw and paint." She shakes her head. "We'll walk the beach . . . the kids will be able to be kids . . . we'll work where there's work; we'll fish, crab, read books, watch storms, make love."

You drop your face into your hands. "There's no work here all winter. And nobody's reading your damn Kate Chopin or listening to your whiny Joan Baez."

She smiles at that. "Oh, we'll get by. I've thought about it. There'll be a lot of money from the sale of the house."

"But I don't want to just get by. I've worked too hard, given up too much to get here."

"Apparently. Well, forget it . . ." She swishes her hand through the air as if swatting a fly and turns her back.

"What?"

"Nothing."

"What?"

She smiles dreamily.

"You know you never made that simpy flower-child smile before you started seeing Dr. Fingeruphisass in Georgetown?"

The smile dissolves and her eyes pool again.

"I'm sorry. I'm sorry. Brenda, sweetheart"—you look around at the cheap panelled walls, the mildewed ceiling, the cracked linoleum—"I just want to go home. That's where my life is. This is . . . vacation."

"Call it what you want, Peter." One hand flies up in the air. "I just can't go back. I need to be here. I need to be at the ocean."

You hold your breath, now watching your wife catch her hair with one hand and snare it with a rubber band; long, long, silky hair, elegant fingers that are tangling you in the nape of her soft neck. "Well, we can't stay here, Brenda." You turn back to the mirror and search the reflection for her disdain. "We just can't."

Shaking her head, she sits down on the bed. Her voice is now as flat as the long beach over the dunes. "I don't know what else to tell you—you're right, Peter, you've heard it all before, but this time I'm not asking." She twists around to look you in the eye, but you have already drifted away in the wind of her voice, your head full of a line in a children's book you used to read to the kids: "I love my house, I love my nest, in all the world my nest is best."

You inhale the damp ocean air. Run your fingers back through your hair. "I guess I don't know what to say anymore. We have to go back." A moment later: "I have to leave." Your scratchy voice is barely audible against the sea, your dark eyes glistening, nostrils suddenly flared. "I'm beat, and there's a lot of work to do before Monday morning. Let's just say that we're leaving at ten."

Standing like a horse backed into a driving squall, Brenda jams the unwilling drawer mostly shut, steps into some old Levi's, jumps up to get them over her hips, buttoned, and zipped, and then walks out of the room, leaving behind a furious thumping in your chest and ears.

Chapter 2

Woody, Michael, and Sarah are sitting behind three cereal boxes placed strategically around the yellow Formica table. They are bickering about who has sole rights to the back seat of the Dodge van for the six-hour trip home when their mother stomps down the narrow hall, stepping into her laceless white Keds, and pushes open the screen door to the deck.

By the time the stretched and rusted spring seems to pause and then finally brings the screen door clapping against the frame, she is already halfway down the wooden steps to the sand eight feet below.

Woody, the baby, a twelve-year-old with his mother's thick hair and olive skin, gets up from the table and runs out the door, leaning over the rail just as she is crossing under the ripped badminton net in front of the cottage. "Mom?" he calls, panic in his cracking voice.

"Woody," she yells from the road, "get back in there and put on a shirt. It's cold!" She continues across the potholed road. "I'll be back later; we'll talk." She moves some hair that has strayed across her teary face. "I'll be back soon. Now go inside. It looks like it might rain. Sarah, would you please take Woody inside?"

Woody is surprised to see his big sister, a junior in high school, standing behind him on the deck. Sarah frowns and puts her arm around his narrow shoulders, leading him—as one does a young colt—through the door that Michael holds open for them, and gives him a pat on his bottom to hurry him up.

Michael, fifteen and neither boy nor man, though already inches taller than you, the ghost of a mustache darkening his upper lip, watches as his sister and brother pass by, catching Sarah's eye accusingly. "What's goin' on?"

"Oh, it's nothing, nothing new anyway," you say from the living room, forcing a smile. Then you turn and step barefoot into the tiny kitchen, green tiles, dark laminated cabinets, toast crumbs on the countertop. "You know Mom; she just doesn't want to go home. She'll be back by ten. I told her that's when we were leaving."

You put on some water for coffee, banging the pot on the sink, sliding it onto the chipped avocado Kenmore. Michael, Woody, and Sarah remain at the screen door. "Just go and get dressed and packed. We'll eat, clean up the place, and then load the van." When you turn they still haven't moved, Woody glancing to Sarah for some direction.

"She'll be back soon," you say.

By 9:55 Brenda has not returned to the boxy cottage up on stilts that she had inherited in 1965 after her grandmother died. You wanted to call it Breezin' Along. Brenda insisted that it had to be Caminada Bay. It was Caminada Bay.

The kids sit at the edge of the worn nubbly couch watching every move you make. After a while you send them over to the beach to find Brenda. "Please tell her that we're leaving. She's probably down by the pier."

At 10:30 the van is packed, the kitchen has been swept in frustrated short bursts, the garbage is taken out, the electricity and water are shut off, the shed beneath the cottage is padlocked. When you pull yourself up to the bare upper deck, splintery handrail by splintery handrail, and scan the low-lying dunes, sea oats waving and leaning to the south, Michael is just then trudging down the sand path followed by Sarah and Woody.

By noon the four of you are sitting cross-legged on the deck under the metal-framed living room windows, eating the stale Twinkies

Brenda had bought for the ride home, staring blankly into the waving dunes.

"When is she gonna be back?" Sarah whines. "I have homework to do tonight. I have to talk to my friends before school tomorrow . . ."

You shrug, glancing first at Michael, who returns the frown as if he is a mirror, and then at Woody, who looks weepy and turns away.

"I have an important practice tomorrow," Michael grumbles.

You close your eyes. "I don't know what to do, kids," you say.

"I have to get back," Michael says. "She can stay here for a few days like she did last year—and take the bus home when she's ready."

Sarah flinches when you slap your hands down on your knees and push yourself up, say, "All right, let's just go. Michael's probably right," even though you know he's wrong.

You cut off Woody's whimpering protest before it forms in his mouth: "I have to be at work at eight o'clock tomorrow morning, bud. Your sister's got homework. And"—you smile—"your brother is being looked at by Dean Smith sometime this week. She'll be fine. She just has to take a bus home. Like she did last year."

The three children look across with their mother's eyes, not knowing what to do. Your eyes are glassy. They've never seen you cry.

Michael has bounded down the rickety steps and is already on the concrete driveway when Sarah gets up. Woody follows silently down the open stairs and steps into the brand-new Dodge van with bikes on the front and rear, a roof rack full of bags, and a red Coleman cooler.

You turn the ignition, take one more long look around at the dunes, and back away from the cottage. Your face feels clammy, that familiar nausea at your throat, the corner of your lip twitching, trembling.

Woody's eyes are on you and then he turns toward Sarah and

leans on her shoulder. "I'm sorry, bud," you say into the mirror.

You jam the shifter into D, and the van jolts down the deserted road. At the Pier Road you check the rearview mirror: three heads turned to the beach. Woody is whimpering loudly enough to hear up in the noisy front.

Your voice is low then like it was sometimes late at night when you'd sit in their rooms before bed: "Don't worry, bud, we're just having an argument. Everybody has arguments. It's natural. Mom'll catch a bus to Norfolk—or rent a car in Manteo—she's done it a bunch of times. In fact, she'll probably be home right after us." You wink in the mirror, but Woody's face is buried in Sarah's shoulder.

CHAPTER 3

The bright blue van moves alone up sand-strewn Highway 12 toward Nags Head, wheels whirring onto the Herbert C. Bonner Bridge over Oregon Inlet. The ocean is whipped up, the gray moving sky all darkness in the hazy distance. The offshore boats haven't gone out, resting like a stormy still life in the marina.

When the first drops of rain splatter on the broad windshield, Sarah blurts out, "Dad, we locked the cottage! She can't even get in!" Her voice lifts at the end like a curtain in the wind.

"She's got a key," you call back.

"She didn't take her purse to the beach!"

You turn your hands from the blue plastic wheel and hold them palms up as if to say *What can I do*?

Woody whines, "Dad, it's raining! And it looks like a big storm."

"It's just rain, Woody. She won't drown. Anyway, this is what Mom wanted—if she didn't she'd have come back. I think this is just like last year. She just needs to stay down here for a couple of days."

So you drive on past the Park Service campground, past the Bodie Island Light, rain pelting the big windshield, on through South Nags Head, wipers on high, and then, just a mile or so before the turn to Manteo on Roanoke Island, you can't stand it any longer, pump the brakes and veer off onto the grass shoulder, slamming the steering wheel with the fat of your hand, shaking your head and clenching your teeth as hard as you can to hold back the torrent of tears that presses for relief.

You wait for a Jeep to pass, then a rusted Chevy stepside pickup that honks just before you swing the van out across the flooded road and lurch back toward the bridge.

It is just past one o'clock when the van pulls in under the small gray cottage with two decks, one stacked unceremoniously on top of the other. Without waiting for the kids, you shoulder out the driver's door, the engine still dieseling, and race two steps at a time to the first deck, wet hair blowing in your eyes, the T-shirt already plastered to your body. The screen door is flapping back and forth in the gusting wind. You grab the knob; it's locked. Then pound on the door yelling her name. Yelling her name. "Bren-daaaaaaaaaa!"

The rain is now moving across the dunes in skidding sheets slapping at your back as you dig deep into faded Levi's for the cottage keys. Fumbling first with finding the right key and then pushing the rusted door open, you scream loud enough to wreck anyone's vocal cords, striding through the small living room and kitchen, ducking quickly into the three tiny bedrooms before smashing your fist into the cedar plank wall. The whole cottage shakes.

When you turn, Sarah is standing in the bedroom doorway. "Is she . . . ?"

"No." Your chest heaves up and down. "No."

You stumble around her, but she follows into the dark living room where you sit down on the edge of the scratched coffee table and bury your face in your hands.

Michael reaches over to turn on the lamp. "The electricity is dead," he grumbles.

No one says a word for a minute, then two minutes. It's been five minutes when Michael picks up an old Spider Man comic from the maple end table, and the three kids lean back into the nubbly cushions, into the dim living room, reading dog-eared magazines, staring around, making silent plans for the next two hours. And wait some more.

"She'll be back," you say. Nobody responds.

* * *

By mid-afternoon the squalls have passed over the narrow barrier island, the sun is perforating the clouds, blinding light slanting through the kitchen window, a magnificent double rainbow out over the ocean. Outside it feels like summer.

You climb to the second deck, followed by the kids, and pace back and forth like a sailor's wife.

Just after 5 p.m., you push yourself up off the rail, finger the indentations on your elbows, and announce that you're going down to the pier to call Nancy Sawyer, Brenda's only real friend on the island. They were classmates at the Cape Hatteras School and went to Chapel Hill when they were freshmen. "She's probably there, I don't know why I didn't think of that earlier."

"Should we come?" Sarah asks.

"No, just wait here in case I'm wrong."

You amble down the deserted strip of sand and gravel to the wind-battered phone booth outside the empty hotel. Nancy's husband Ray answers and you say only that Brenda has gone out and you're looking for her. But Sawyer is no help. He has been down in Buxton all day—and tells you that Nancy has gone to Chapel Hill to visit her sister Addie, who is pregnant. He makes a stale joke about the "two of us counting our blessings" and hangs up.

With nowhere else to turn, you drop another dime in the slot and call Bruce Hill at his trailer down in Salvo. The Dare County Sheriff is eating, chewing loudly on something like an apple as he listens patiently to your ramblings about Brenda's possible whereabouts. But when he hears that there'd been "a little argument," he smacks his lips and says, "You call me back in the mornin' if she don't return. She always was a hothead, I remember." Bruce was a couple of years ahead of her at the Cape Hatteras School.

"What should I do till then?"

"Feed your kids. Then go to sleep. She'll be back. They gen'ly don't stay mad long."

* * *

After the dry bologna sandwiches and cookies, the kids refuse to go to bed that evening, sprawling out on the living room floor, reading the same old comics left on the dusty unpainted shelves, playing solitaire with sticky dog-eared composite decks, staring out the rattling screens, listening to the incessant moan of the wind across the narrow island. When the last one—Michael—falls asleep on the rug, you move a rocker out onto the deck and wait there shivering until dawn.

At first light you slip in and out of the cottage and run over the dunes and then down to the pier. There are three old coots leaning on the scarred railing, eyes on their lines way out in the frothy surf. None of them has seen a woman on the beach, but you can't help but see the smirk in their shaking mugs and already hear the guffaws that will come as you race back to the pay phone to wake Bruce Hill.

Then you call work. Then the kids' schools with a lie about car problems.

Within an hour Sheriff Hill has gathered a small posse of National Park Service Rangers and volunteer firemen and their wives—and they spend all of Monday, a warm, almost windless day, scouring the marshes and dunes, the seemingly endless stretches of nothing but sand and water.

And find nothing. Not a sweatshirt. No sneakers. Two North Carolina State Police come knocking at the cottage door early that night asking the same questions Bruce Hill had asked at 6:30 in the morning, a cup of coffee and a cigarette in his chubby hand.

* * *

Tuesday is a smudged mirror of Monday. Streaked and dirty on Wednesday, and grimier still on Thursday. And so for dateless days tripping end on end like dried sea grass down a windy beach, the search for Brenda Hudson goes on, Woody moaning to himself, the wind sweeping the empty shoreline. Sarah and Michael, pained beyond speech, give up the search earlier and earlier each day, returning to the cottage to pore over the same old magazines and to play solitaire, poker, gin, hearts, anything that will fill the time before they can go to sleep again.

You hold Woody's small hand as the two of you walk the silent miles along an unchanging coast, sit with him in the dunes, tell him old family stories designed to make the boy smile, all the while looking for some clue—anything—that will lead the family out of this island desert.

Now it seems that the only thing out of place on the entire unruly three-town stretch of beach is Elvin Midgett's pontoon boat, which he noticed was gone the day Brenda was reported missing. It's a general cause for speculation—and maybe some ill-conceived solace—but as Elvin admits when he sobers up, it might have been blown away a week before during another big storm.

So each morning you wake early, before the kids, and scuttle across the dunes like a ghost crab to make sure that Brenda's corpse hasn't washed up during the night.

And each evening, after another solemn and overcooked dinner of macaroni and cheese or spaghetti and Ronzoni tomato sauce, you leave the cottage without explanation. The kids don't ask, just watch you turn from the sink full of dishes and go the quarter mile down to the pay phone and dial the familiar number—20, 30, 40 rings in the empty kitchen in the empty house in northern Virginia—and then walk back to the quiet cottage, fall into the nubbly worn couch where Woody leans under your weary arm as if it were a warm cave into which he curls himself to sleep. Only then will you carry the boy into the small room he shares with his brother.

And only then will Sarah get up, walk down the hall, and enter the darkness of her bedroom, leaving you alone with Michael, who plays game after game of solitaire on the coffee table, dealing single hands long past midnight, eventually lapsing into sleep right where he sits on the couch.

And when the cottage finally ceases its nightly whimpering, the wind shaking the pilings beneath everyone, you turn off the lights and sit with a beer or a coffee, a Lucky Strike burning in a clam ashtray, wondering what has become of your wife, your family, the life you once thought you enjoyed.

By the end of the second week, an unwieldy despair replacing the edgy tick in your heart, you finally decide—or perhaps find some anguished comfort in believing—that Brenda has simply run away in order to keep the family from returning to Rosslyn. She's hiding out somewhere. There is just no other explanation. She certainly wouldn't have gone swimming; it was too cold, too rough, and she knew better. And despite her great admiration for Edna Pontellier, she wouldn't have given herself up to the sea. Not Brenda. Brenda never gave in.

"We don't have a clue," mutters the sheriff the following Sunday after his small department has tried searching the beach down in Avon, dropping a lit cigarette in the hot sand and burying it with his brown shoe. "It's none o' my business, Pete, but why 'on't you take those chilrun back to their home. There ain't nothin' here but pain for 'em."

You nod, knowing the man is right, but what can you do? And when you turn and walk back to the van, the kids are already in their seats.

On the long way back to the cottage, with Sarah sitting in Brenda's seat, you speak to the two boys in the rearview mirror, the wind whistling through the passenger window open a crack. "It's time to go home, kids. It's been two weeks. I don't know if there's any point in . . ." You can't finish.

No one says a word, not even Sarah. Maybe there's nothing left to say, you think, just the plain truth as you turn the van into the narrow concrete driveway and cut the engine. The kids get out and you speak to the empty van. "I think she's run off. I think she's still around here. I think this is her way of making us stay here."

That's what you're going to say when you get back into the cottage. But as you step through the door, Sarah is waiting for you, biting the inside of her cheek, telling you out of the side of her mouth, "We talked about it, Dad, me and Michael—and Woody too—and we decided we're not going to leave. We can't." She swallows a moan and turns away. "How could we leave her?"

"She left us, Sarah."

Sarah opens her face to you then, flushed and now flowing over with tears. "It's all your fault!" she wails. "It's all your fault. I hate you!"

And you reach for her trembling shoulders, to bring her close under your unshaven chin, to bury her anguished expression, to rock her softly back and forth as you once did when she was a little girl. But she grows rigid in your arms, her slender hands pushing on your chest until you drop your hands, stuffing them into your pockets, and Sarah falls to the floor sobbing.

The lonely walk over to the pier is made lonelier by the cold wind just now coming from the north. All you can do is lean over the rail, watch the waves rushing one by one by one, endlessly against the pilings beneath your feet. An hour later Sarah is sitting cross-legged on the deck as you walk slowly down the dark, potholed lane. She is wearing that thick hooded sweatshirt from UNC that Brenda used to wear on the weekends. After you climb the rickety steps and ask if she wants company, she shrugs and you sit down beside her, leaning back hard on the rough cedar shakes. The boys are nowhere in sight.

When you put your arm around her, she leans into the hollow beneath your shoulder. "I'm sorry," you whisper. "I just don't know what to do."

"She's dead, Dad. I know she's dead," she says, her lower lip trembling like a two-year-old.

"She's not dead, Sarah. I know that. I'd know. I can still feel her around us. She's still in my heart."

Sarah shakes her head. "I know she went in the water, Dad—that's what she does when things get too crazy for her.

She went in the water and got swept out by a riptide."

"I don't think so, baby girl. You know how cold the water is in April. Besides, they would have found something left behind, her jeans, her red sweatshirt, something."

Something.

"Something," Sarah mumbles and shifts her head.

The two of you sit like that leaning on the cottage wall long after it is dark, until Michael and Woody finally come out and say they're starving.

Chapter 4

As April surrenders to May, one day separated only by darkness into the next, you emerge from sleeplessness each early morning and tiptoe out of the cottage. On the deck you yank on sneakers and then follow the path across the sand over to the beach, standing for a few seconds in the sea oats at the top of the dune, scanning the vast emptiness of sky and water, the long arc between heaven and earth. Day after day. Week after week.

This early morning ritual quickly becomes so rigid, so habitual, rain or shine, cold or early-summer heat, that you can't remember what you used to do in the mornings on Hatteras before Brenda disappeared. Every morning running hard north to the pier, then walking and running farther north about two miles to the edge of the Pea Island National Seashore, then back south toward the pier, continuing on two miles or so through Waves to the Salvo line. And then the three mile return.

It's a way of making sure that you can check the beach before the increasingly warm mornings wake the kids earlier and earlier. It is also a way of letting go of all those emptied nights, the insomniac's dreams, the memories, Woody climbing into your bed; the need, derision, scorn, pain, all sweated out in an hour back and forth. Every early morning.

Exactly two months to the day that Brenda walked out of the cottage for the last time, the Park Service officially gives up the search. The State Police have had her description out for thirty days. She has not washed up on the beach. No one remembers seeing her at all that day except the family. And, aside from Woody, who has thought he's spotted her (way, way, way down the beach) maybe once a week, waving and screaming until Sarah or you could reel him into your arms, there is not even a trace of her left behind.

Nothing. Nothing. Nothing. Unless you consider Elvin Midgett's sailboat. Nothing. A flutter of wind. That flutter of wind.

Elbows on the counter down at the Salvo Market, you mention that insignificant flutter to John Barnes, but Barnes is too busy packing bloodworms to pay you any mind. *Nor'easters are jes' facts a life 'round here, Mr. Bigshit Virginia* he may have been thinking moments before you lower your face into your arms and start to weep.

On the 21st of June, having used all your vacation and sick days, you call the office back in Falls Church and make the only arrangements you can: a six-month unpaid leave of absence. No guarantees after that. "That's the best we can do, Peter. I'm sorry this has happened, but you must understand our position. It's really a bad break for all of us."

"Fuck you," you mumble and hang up, tears blurring your eyes as you kick the bottom panel of the phone booth near the empty hotel and trot back down the road to the cottage.

Just before you reach the cottage, Woody comes racing over the dunes screaming and yelling as if he had seen a ghost. "I saw her!! I saw her!! This time I really saw her!!" He points back behind him. Sarah and Michael burst from the door and race down to meet him.

The twelve-year-old is still shrieking, his face white as the belly of a fish, sobbing and gasping, trying to catch his breath. Sarah holds him tight enough that he can still direct them into the van and over to the sandy road in front of Raymond Sawyer's grocery and tackle shop. "There!" he cries. "There! There! Down there!"

You step on the gas and fishtail all the way down the narrow lane until the pavement disappears into sand and you pull over on the side near the empty KOA as everyone bursts from the three doors of the van and races toward the high dune screaming her name, screaming her names, one by one clambering to the top of the dune to find nothing, the same nothing: empty sky, empty beach. Two old fishermen surf casting and a youngish couple walking hand in hand maybe a quarter mile down.

Panting, trying to slow your breath, you stand in front of the old guys, demand to know if they have seen a woman walking the beach, reach into your pocket and pull out a wrinkly photograph of Brenda on the neat lawn back in Rosslyn.

The old man shakes his head and looks to his friend, who just shrugs, a mean smirk glinting at the edge of his thin tobacco stained mouth.

"But I saw her!! I saw her!!" your baby boy pleads as he crumbles into the sand and the two other kids turn and walk away into the dunes. Your chest is heaving, a wail stuck in your throat like a fish bone as you turn slowly around and around and around like some pitiful old drunk, dropping flat on your back to the sand where the earth and the sky become one. And belly-up to the gods, you weep openly like your poor forlorn boy Woody down the beach, because it just doesn't matter anymore. It doesn't matter anymore whether Brenda is dead or alive. She isn't coming back. The wind blows like wild horses racing along an empty beach with nowhere to go.

* * *

Brenda was a young freshman, still seventeen and just arrived in Chapel Hill from Rodanthe, when you saw her standing in front of the Old Well. You told everyone that you fell in love with her in that moment: her long hair and her silky browned skin and her dark eyes, the swaybacked slope of her thin hips, her long graceful fingers.

She was obviously lost; a little annoyed, it seemed. Maybe scared. And now your daughter Sarah stands in front of you daily with the same confused, almost angry look, the darkness under her cheekbones, the untamed swells behind her eyes, the same steadfast refusal toward the end of August to return home to Rosslyn until she knows for certain what has happened to her mother. Michael and Woody stand right behind her.

"We won't go, Dad," she says. "No matter what you—" She doesn't finish.

Your will is now long past broken, and you close your burning eyes and agree to stay, ". . . for a year . . . at most." And at the end of August, you enroll the children in the K-12 Cape Hatteras School in Buxton—where their mother had gone to school—using the same public relations skills Brenda hated to convince Principal Covey to put the kids in their proper grades, despite not having finished the term in Rosslyn.

Then you begin looking for ways to scrape out a living on the island.

For a man who had been mid-stride in building a successful career in advertising for Gaynor, Kotcher, Russek and Associates in Falls Church, you soon find there is little work anywhere on the Outer Banks during off-season. It takes just three calls from the pay phone down by the pier to determine that there is no ad agency for a hundred miles, that there is already an alcoholic ex-newspaperman from Akron who is selling airtime on the barrier islands' only radio station, and the closest daily newspaper is up in Elizabeth City.

So one sleepless night—no different than all the rest—alone on the deck in a cancerous-looking folding beach chair with Schlitz in one hand and five others at your feet, you turn to the now nightly memory of your lost wife walking down the narrow hall and, because there are no other options, acquiesce to her nonsensical, dreamy idea of publishing a weekly newspaper.

And once you enter Brenda's dream, you are swept along like a piece of driftwood in a starless reverie of press passes and scoops and investigative forays into missing persons and Mencken-like editorials about men and women until the six-pack is empty and you drift off to an alcoholic sleep in the beach chair.

At first groggy light, looking around at the potholed road and the few nondescript cottages, you push your cold, aching body up to take your morning run over the dunes and down the beach, and the dream suddenly seems as flimsy as the pitted aluminum beach chair you fling over the rail.

But a day later you find an old Royal portable at a used office furniture place in Elizabeth City. Speak to a printer there, and convince him to barter the cost of the first printing for a full-page ad. And on the way home you borrow a 1959 journalism textbook from the library on Fernando Street in Manteo.

* * *

The first issue of *The Island Weekly* comes out in October featuring a sophomorically upbeat story about the biggest real estate office on Hatteras, a two-person operation out of Buxton; half the piece was made up as you sat bleary-eyed and fingers twitching at the old Royal trying to fill space. The paper barely filled up eight pages (two sheets front and back), half of which was more advertising that you sold to businesses that couldn't possibly benefit from an ad until the next round of tourists returned in the spring.

The *Weekly*, as it is soon called by the natives, doesn't bring in much money at first—in fact almost nothing—but it is enough to get by in a place where there is very little to do besides fish and walk the beach. Mostly it fills your time. There is a lot of driving to be done; talking to local folks to get something to write about, creating classifieds, selling ads with the lure of some future feature story, picking up the stacks in Elizabeth City and personally distributing bundles of papers every Wednesday from way up in Kitty Hawk nearly eighty miles down to the Ocracoke ferry. Meanwhile, your children are burying their grief in the monotony of school days in Buxton, where their suburban Virginia ways briefly make them the focus of unwarranted attention, the ridicule and scorn that trails all outsiders.

After the bus drops them off on the ocean side of Highway 12 each day, the three kids pretty much spend all afternoon working on *The Island Weekly*. Sarah is the assistant editor. She also covers the various town meetings so you can stay home with Woody, who still cries himself to sleep every night.

Michael, who turns sixteen in September, but glumly refuses a birthday party or cake, follows Island sports. (He had been the starting point guard on the Rosslyn High varsity as a freshman—and is already a star "prospect" at Cape Hatteras School.)

And so you move along through the colorless beach fall into winter, nor'easters, an occasional snow squall blowing across from the Sound, power out, flying snow blurring the distinctions between concrete and deep sand shoulders, cars stuck for hours off the side of the road, cold bitchy nights, the cottage rocking on its stilts, kids staring up at the ceiling each night, alone in their beds, waiting for the warm humid breezes again, waiting for sleep to overcome memory.

Part II: 1973

Chapter 5

The first time Jessica Dneiper Walsh shows up at Caminada Bay, you think she's kind of pushy, a quirky smile on her face as she jumps up and down there on the other side of the steel door after a freak January blizzard, snow blowing off the roof in swirls, a crumb cake from the North Beach Campground in her outstretched hands like a sacrificial offering. "Hey, I just thought y'all might need some company and . . ."

You hardly know the woman. Just that she is the English teacher at the Cape Hatteras School—Sarah and Michael's teacher.

You met briefly at the Fall Open House where she asked you to stick around for a quick conference.

That evening, Jessica told you that your senior girl and sophomore boy were too quiet and too polite—and way too suburban—for their own good on that rough and windy barrier island. She said she managed to get Sarah to talk to her once or twice for a few minutes at lunch about Rosslyn and what her life was like back there in Virginia when everything was different. But that was all. Sarah had closed her eyes against Jessica's gentle questions and made up transparent excuses to get to class or the library to find a book.

Michael is, in the English teacher's parlance, a closed book altogether. Everything was "okay." "I'm okay." "Really. Okay. Okay?" "I don't think about Rosslyn much at all, Miss Walsh." All he seems to care about is basketball.

So on the January night she shows up at the cottage, Michael and Sarah are stunned by the vision of their English teacher framed in the door, both likely assuming they have done something wrong, another shovelful of sand tossed in their faces.

But as you are soon to find out, after a harsh fall in her own life, Jessica Walsh has picked herself up out of an unhappy funk and decided to help "the poor Hudsons" through their grief—and the long lonely winter out in front of everyone on the island. You are going to be her winter project, in place of quilting or writing the great American island novel or finally reading Proust.

When the kids disappear behind their bedroom doors, twice assured they are not being punished for anything, she says *sotto voce* that Sarah looks so forlorn sitting stoop shouldered in her English class day after day that she "just couldn't stand around seeing a kid like that."

She says she figures it's lonely enough all winter on Hatteras without missing your mother, especially in the middle of an unlikely storm.

So with snow swirling all around, she showed up at the rusted door, jumping up and down on the windy deck. It's the first time anyone besides police has knocked on the door. It is also the first time you hear the name Buddy Neuse—and how Jessica thinks Sarah might be sweet on him. And vice versa.

She tells you not to believe all the gossipy warnings about Buddy. Beneath the rough Islander surface, she thinks he has a good heart.

* * *

Five months later, driving up Highway 12 to Manteo to catch a bus to Norfolk, you think Sarah looks like a little girl in the driver's seat, her bare foot barely reaching the gas pedal. Without a word, both hands on the blue plastic steering wheel, she drives the thirty or so miles to Roanoke Island and drops you off at the new Ace Hardware. She offers her cheek like an annoyed wife in a Ford

Country Squire at the Rosslyn train station when you lean over to kiss her good-bye.

"It'll be all right," you say. She stares straight ahead at the pink building and shakes her head. "I promise."

The old yellowed school bus to Norfolk, a Trailways to Washington, and then a ridiculously expensive cab ride to a Hertz outlet make the six-hour trip nearly twelve hours.

"In Rosslyn Hills, Virginia," as you wrote in *The Island Weekly* to fill space a week later, "the quarter-acre lawns resemble the air-brushed photos on the front of Scott Seed packages: newly mowed, deep green, weed free, thick, cool, and very, very, very soft under-foot. Watered daily by underground sprinkling systems, tended weekly by brown-skinned gardeners, and treated monthly with chemical fertilizers, the yards are far more perfect than the in-habitants inside the modest tract homes. When an intruder steps off the flagstone path, footprints remain in the bent grass as proof of the trespass into the hybridized nature that covers the terrain around the ranches and split-levels which blossomed there in the early '50s."

The next day, you leave the absurdly formal closing held in the conference room at the Rosslyn branch of First Federal Savings Bank without a handshake—in fact, you never even looked at the Jameses, Marsha and Jim, who have bought the house for a lot less than you and Brenda thought it was worth—and then drive slowly out of the village and over to the Queen's Woods Development.

Turning the car onto Potomac Lane, you signal needlessly and roll up to the driveway at number 14, stopping inches before the ga-rage door. For a moment, sunlight splotching your vision, bursting light showers in front of your eyes, you think you might faint; a few moments later you are on the flagstone path without remembering getting out of the car, one dusty wing-tipped shoe in front of the other.

No one is out on the street, not a soul out on their lawns. You swivel around like a soldier and stare across at the Weils' house, wondering whether they are watching from behind their living room drapes.

* * *

You had returned to Rosslyn once before during the previous fall just to get the kids' clothes and papers and hidden cash you desperately needed from the safe-deposit box, but you weren't ready or even really interested in staying around that time. In an hour or less you were in and out of the musty house—running out of the place like you had once raced up out of the dark cellar when you were a kid in Charlotte, heart thudding, pins and needles in your fingers—so relieved to hear the click of the door behind you, to hear the van's engine turn over, to hear the AM radio fill the quivering spaces.

And when you got home to Rodanthe on that hot evening in late September, west wind blowing flies in from the marshes, Sarah and Woody were waiting on the deck, Woody's hand up in the air, the sun going down over Pamlico Sound. Woody raced down the steps and pressed himself into your embrace. But Sarah stood at the landing and watched, just as Brenda might have done, as Woody and you walked hand in hand up the creaking steps to her perch.

You remember how you asked for Michael, but Sarah just shook her head, brought her hands to her eyes and pointed behind her into the cottage.

You found Michael sitting on the brown pilly couch dealing a game of solitaire, one of the five pointless versions he played night after night before bed. He didn't look up, so you ambled over and plopped yourself down with a groan beside the tall and lanky boy, rubbed his bent back like you used to do back in Rosslyn before anything went wrong. "So, bud, I brought some things back for you from the house."

Michael nodded and kept turning over cards.

"Do you want to see them?"

"Not now," the boy mumbled, "I'll um . . ." He moved a red queen onto a black king and pressed his thin lips together. "I'll just look through the stuff later." He glanced up. "Okay?"

"It was hard to be back there, bud, a lot harder than I figured . . . but I gotta tell you, it's nice to be back here with you and Sarah and Woody."

Michael seemed to shrug and then swept the cards together with both hands, standing up and walking over to the sink where he turned on the tap and leaned over to slurp up the hissing water. A few seconds later he had already wiped his mouth with his forearm, walked down the dark hall, and disappeared into his small bedroom.

You remember how you glanced across at Sarah, who had stepped into the cottage unnoticed, but she waved you off and turned to go outside on the deck again.

You followed her. What else was there to do? She was sitting cross-legged on the porch swing staring across at the desolate dunes, the rusted chain squeaking with each insignificant move of her thin body.

"Why won't he speak to me, Sarah?"

"I don't know, Dad." A scowl twisted her face. "I already told you, he doesn't really speak to me, either." The blue sky streaked with orange. Three brown pelicans soaring just above the water.

"He can't still think that I'm to blame for Mom's disappearing?"

She turned her head and glared straight into your eyes.

"Does he?"

"You'll have to ask him."

But Michael just lay on his bed, hands behind his head, staring up at the wainscot ceiling, when you got up the courage with a shot of Jim Beam and sat down on the narrow bed with him later that evening.

"I want you to know that I'm so sorry, Michael, that I left her—Mom—on the beach that morning. You have to know that I have never forgiven myself. You must know that I've regretted it every waking moment since we got back here that afternoon and found the cottage empty. It's probably the worst thing that I've ever done . . . and Lord knows I've done some pretty bad things in my life. I just felt so trapped, I didn't know what to do next."

You sat down on the bed then, your hand flat on the pillow next to the boy's head, inflamed pimples on his broad forehead. "I'm sorry, Michael."

"Well, I'm sorry, too, Dad," Michael said dryly and sat up. "I guess I'm gonna take a walk." He swiveled his feet off the mattress, but before he could step away, you grabbed him by the wrist. "Michael, please talk to me. Please tell me what you're thinking about for God's sake!"

The boy glared at you then. "Well, believe it or not, I'm not thinking about anything." he said, twisting his hand in the vice. "All I'm thinking about is walking down to the pier." You held on tightly to his bony wrist, but he pulled himself away.

"Michael, wait . . . I am sorry for putting you through this now—but I just have to get straight with you before I lose you, too."

Michael clenched his teeth. "I am not going anywhere." He pulled away with his arm like a boat tethered to a dock." I'm just walking down the road. There's nothing to get straight. I'll be back."

You took a deep breath and let it out very slowly. "You know that your mom was very unhappy, don't you, Michael? She was always dissatisfied with—"

Michael shook his head and yanked himself free, striding out the door and holding his freed hand up behind him like a shield. The cottage shuddered as he took staccato steps down the wooden stairs, away from everyone and everything he used to know—and anyone who used to know him.

And you remained sitting on the bed until it grew dark in the room, your hot face pressed into your open palms; and then suddenly—or at least it felt suddenly—you pushed yourself up and walked into the lamplit living room where Sarah and Woody were silently rummaging through the overstuffed duffel bags, making four piles of clothes.

* * *

Now, more than a year after Brenda strode out of the cottage for an angry walk, you are back in Rosslyn, standing in the living room of a furnished house uninhabited all that time. You leave a fingerprint on everything you touch.

On the filmy upright piano you see the eight-by-ten photograph of the family taken in 1960, just after Woody was born. You pick up the frame, rub the dust off on your pant leg, and look. Sarah and Michael are on either side of their serenely smiling mother, who is holding her newborn. You are behind them, arms spread wide, hands resting on Sarah's and Michael's shoulders.

Everything in the photograph is perfect; it reminds you of a picture one would see in *LIFE* magazine of an astronaut or some pop singer like Perry Como relaxing with his family on the weekend.

You wipe the glass once more with your sleeve and try to place the frame exactly the way it had been during the entire year, the way children try to walk in others' footsteps along the shore.

Wandering then—more as a customer or a rental agent than an owner—through the rest of the house, there is a metallic taste of the flu in your mouth. Your muscles and joints plead for an hour or two on the couch.

The worst of it, you imagine, will be going through Brenda's closet and drawers, taking what you can for Sarah—who will instantly hate you for bringing her mother back to her like that in bags, but will never forgive you if you don't.

You have already envisioned some of it as if you were in a movie, holding her thin silk bras and panties in your trembling hands, tossing them into the garbage pile, weeping deep into the night.

And when you are done doing exactly what you imagined you would, you return to the living room simply to look at the photograph once more. In this light, it seems that Brenda's beautiful eyes, blue as a robin's egg, are dappled with remorse, not serenity. And now you recall those first angry and despairing weeks of Woody's life, the way they really were, not as they appear in the beautiful picture.

How many nights had you stayed up until dappled dawn, leaning back onto the headboard of your rumpled bed, cigarettes flowing over the edge of the glass ashtray, talking and talking and talking, as if by going over the same thing, the same questions, the same betrayals over and over again, something would click for her. Always, always, always she assured him it had nothing to do with him. "It's me alone, Peter, I just can't seem to get straight with the world. I feel out of place everywhere I go."

And as you turn away toward the bedrooms, the sensation of the frame's ridges still on your fingertips, you wonder how Woody can stand looking at the photograph of Brenda thumbtacked on the wall next to his pillow at the cottage. The boy lies there every night, head turned toward the wall, waiting for the smiling woman to walk in off the warm spring beach, long hair blowing in a calm breeze, just waiting for her to call his name and gather him in her arms and tell him everything is all right again.

But you know that photograph is a lie, too. You had taken the snapshot two days before Brenda disappeared and were surprised to see it nearly six months later when you finally had the roll of film developed up in Kitty Hawk. On a fifty-something degree day on the beach, the wind howling like a hammer, blowing sand down from the pier, Brenda had insisted on taking her winter coat off before you clicked the shutter. And that image is thumbtacked on Woody's wall.

Now you stand outside Woody's room, a homemade NO TRESPASSING sign on the door. Pushing the unlatched door open, you see the new furniture you had forgotten about: the fancy oak desk, the sailboat wallpaper, the painted shelves full of toys and games, the posters of horses and baseball players.

And as you lie down on the dusty quilt, you slowly scan the walls as if cataloging everything in the room. On one shelf is a game that seemed to have a cellophane wrapper still in place. CLUE. A present from the last Christmas you were all together. Unopened. Now you're crying again, a deep mourning kind of moan for your wife and for your poor boy, as if he, too, had died on the beach.

You stumble out of your son's perfect room, heart thumping as you pass your own bedroom down the hall, knocking your shin on the coffee table in the living room and falling onto the couch.

* * *

Early the next morning you splash some cold water on your face and drive a half hour over to a diner in Arlington so you won't see anyone you know. You sit in a booth way in the back of the glitzy place, read every word in *The Washington Post*, do most of the crossword puzzle, have four refills on the coffee, and at noon drive home on the beltway to meet a furniture dealer back at the house.

That afternoon you pack what Sarah, Woody, and Michael wanted or needed, call UPS to pick it up, phone the Salvation Army to cart away the rest, and then sit by yourself with your memories on a folding lawn chair on the dusty, leafy screened porch until it is dusk, peepers scratching the eyes out of the day.

Chapter 6

And then here she is again, Jessica Walsh, standing on the curb at the Norfolk airport, twinkling blue eyes and a toothy smile that could melt memories packed in dry ice. You didn't ask her to come.

Carrying two bags apiece, you struggle through the sweltering heat toward the beat-up Jeep Cherokee she had parked under a tree. The heaviest suitcase is Woody's, full of junk from a very detailed list made by the boy whose voice is suddenly cracking so comically that it provides practically the only laughter you can share with your older children.

Jessica drops the suitcases and reaches into her Mexican bag. A moment later, a ring of keys is flying at your chest. You drop the bags and reach out into the hot air, but they fall clinking to the ground. "What . . . ?"

"You don't think I'm gonna drive you home, too?"

You laugh a little uneasily, still confused what Jessica's unexpected appearance is all about. Maybe it just doesn't matter.

The heat in the Jeep is almost unbearable, even after opening up all the windows and driving out of the parking lot. At the first traffic light, you glance over at Jessica, her bare foot up on the dashboard, blond hair falling from the nest of a ponytail and translucent pearls of sweat on her forehead and upper lip. The extra-large white T-shirt from Jobob's Texaco hangs on her tanned and slightly freckled shoulders.

Still in her early thirties, she has a sensual athletic body, smooth and muscular legs, long elegant fingers—just like Brenda's. Alone at night with your beers, you have often wondered why she is not married. You know that there is not a man on Hatteras—maybe anywhere—who would not do almost anything for the devotion of a woman like Jessica Walsh.

And in the short time that you have known her she has been seemingly that devoted to you and your children, calling, showing up unexpectedly with a cake or ice cream, at first as a pretense to see Sarah or to drop off a letter to the editor or to play a game of Scrabble . . . and later on with no pretense at all, just to be there as you and the kids stumble through the healing that seems to have no end. What salvation, what consolation does she find in your splintered existence?

As you drive onto 64 East toward Chesapeake, you are tempted to reach over and grasp her slender hand, but shoo that thought away the way you chase one of those deer flies, then grab the big wheel tight in your fists, bearing down on the pavement, your forehead bursting with sweat.

Back in April Jessica had invited you over for a "quiet evening" away from the kids. The two of you drank a lot of bad red wine and danced on the linoleum floor to some scratched records from the '50s, got drunk and sloppy and held hands and stayed up all night. She told you then about the Island gossip going around about the family after Brenda disappeared—including the rumors that you had murdered Brenda, or that Brenda had run off with a Negro handyman, or that there was some insurance scam going on.

You rambled on and on that night about Brenda and how much you hurt and how sometimes you were afraid that you might never let go of the ache, it felt so bad—and sometimes so good. It was better than nothing.

Your head in her lap, the ceiling swirling slowly around, she told you some of her secrets, too. About the young husband she had lost in a car accident in 1968; about the parents who abandoned each other and then her to bourbon and pack after pack of Pall Malls; about her anchor, her grandfather PawPaw, who no longer recognized her when she saw him.

And when she finally leaned down and kissed you as the sun slipped through the dusty living room window the following morning, you, who had spent the night yearning for her soft lips on yours, felt nothing but fingers around your dry throat, the blood draining from your buzzing skull, chin pressed into the neck of her T-shirt like some thirteen-year-old, mumbling something like you had to get right home before the kids woke up.

Jessica held her hair off her face, eyes teary and wide, and you realized that no man had ever said no to her before. She pressed her trembling lips together in a smile. She touched your bloodless face with a soft palm and said she understood. And maybe she did. But for how long?

* * *

It is already mid-afternoon when you get back to Caminada Bay. You mumble something about having work to do. As soon as the worn brakes on the Jeep squeal to a stop on the narrow concrete drive in front of the cottage, Jessica jumps out, yanks off her white T-shirt, drops her shorts, and, adjusting her white bikini top and bottom, runs across the hot sand.

You watch her disappear over the dunes like a man trapped in an iron lung, unable to lift your arms or raise your voice above a whisper.

You have only enough strength to take one bag at a time up the wobbly steps to the empty cottage. Four trips up and down, your shirt soaked through like you'd been standing in a driving squall, getting dizzy and nauseous, the cottage closing in around your swirling head, you lie down on the couch.

Fifteen minutes later, you force yourself over to the cluttered Formica table and start typing on the battered Royal, punching out a cookie-cutter editorial off the top of your head about the "senseless" liquor laws in the backwards state of North Carolina.

An hour after that you are wiping the sweat out of your eyes with the tips of your fingers when Jessica walks in with your faded bathing suit (which she had taken off the line), throws it over the typewriter, and says you have to come down to the water. She says she can't enjoy herself while you're slaving away. "It's crazy to work now, Peter. Give yourself a day off. It'll still be there tomorrow." She adds a little patronizingly, "It won't go away, Peter. It never goes away, but God, it's hot out there."

"Sometimes I think this is all I have."

"That's crazy, too." She frowns. "You have a lot more than that. Now, go get your suit on before I rip your clothes off and dress you myself."

It not only sounds like she is talking to a small child, but minutes later she is leading you by the hand like a three-year-old over the path, across the hot dunes, and down to the cooler sand near the incoming tide.

No one is on the beach. Not even the kids. The two of you are all alone in the vast sandy expanse, broken only by the pier.

She points to the towel and tells you to lie down on your stomach, her soft thighs around your waist, that luscious flank in the small of your back, her hands kneading some cool aloe into your aching shoulders.

The aloe and her strong hands feel so good that your eyes fill and your lip starts trembling. You had thought that you would never cry again after packing Brenda's things away the day before. But here it is again, moving in like the tide just then washing your outstretched feet, Jessica lying along the length of you, breasts pressed into your back, soft hands gliding down your outstretched arms.

And you turn over and wrap your arms around her bare shoulders with such affection and gratitude that she has to lean back to push her lips against yours, her soft palms cradling your face, her tongue in the darkness of your halting moan, your hands sliding down her soft, naked back to the slope of her bottom.

She tilts her head back. "Hey," she says with the same shy smirk you saw in Norfolk, "I think we're about to give them all something to talk about around here."

But you hold up your hand. "Not yet. Not yet. I'm just not ready to go public with all this."

She rises up on her haunches, leans over to kiss you coolly on the forehead, stands and walks slowly back to the dunes.

And when the tide finally does what it seemingly intended all along, suddenly washing over your feet and then the towel, you scramble in vain to get out of its way.

You wring out the towel, brush the wet sand off your legs, and decide it's time to find the kids and tell them what happened back in Rosslyn.

Chapter 7

A tired westerly ruffles the graying curtains over a sink full of listing plastic bowls and a burned pot caked with two-day-old Kraft Macaroni and Cheese. Scanning the kitchen for a towel that probably hasn't been hanging anywhere near there for more than a year, you wipe your hands on your shorts and turn around to face your children. The green linoleum feels cool on your bare feet.

Sarah, Michael, and Woody are sitting stiffly around the wobbly Formica table waiting for an "important family meeting." The last important meeting was when you told the kids about going up to Crouse Arnot's law office in Manteo and having their mother declared legally dead.

You wait patiently, as if you're preparing to make a presentation for an advertising promotion back in Rosslyn, until each child is looking your way, Michael being the last. "So, as you might imagine, it was very difficult, but the trip to Rosslyn went very well . . . the house was sold to a nice young family, and I got everything important packed away. The rest went to the Salvation Army."

You see the children holding their breaths as you feel your cheeks begin to crumple with the tics and tremors that precede tears, but you close your eyes tightly against the deluge, and somehow manage to put your face back together the way that they know it. "I have to tell you," you begin, but Sarah interrupts, as if a piece of memory like flotsam has just floated by. She asks about Beth and then in rapid succession about Suzy, Robin, Caroline.

"Was anyone on the street?" Woody asks, not waiting to hear

about Sarah's friends.

"Nope."

"Did you see Robert or Jason?"

"Woody, Sarah"—you smile, lower lip trembling—"I didn't see anyone. No one. Just Marlo. She sold the house."

Now you check with Michael—suddenly noticing the dark fuzz on his upper lip—but Michael looks bored.

"Well," you start again, anxious to get away from Michael's contemptuous stare, "The good part of all this is the old house is sold and we have a lot more money than we did two days ago. So I think we should celebrate by going out to dinner up in Kill Devil Hills at Evan's Crab House." Adding in as offhand a manner as possible, "Maybe Jessica Walsh will come along to help us celebrate."

No one says a word. But after some throat clearing and forearm scratching, Woody asks finally if you found a note "or anything" from their mother, and then waits for an explanation that would make it all make sense.

For those few seconds no one moves. The four of you just sit there, elbows on the sticky Formica, until you break the spell: "I'm sorry, bud. I'm sorry for all of us. But I packed a suitcase for each of you—most of the things you put on your list and a few other odds and ends I thought you might want. The rest I shipped parcel post. They'll get here in a week or two. Or three." You force a weak smile at Woody. "You know Hatteras."

Sarah nods as the pot of water on the stove begins to boil, and you rise and ask them, "Sanka?"

Woody giggles at the question, and Sarah waves you off with an annoyed Brenda gesture. Michael just looks out the window as you pour the instant coffee directly from the jar into the cup and then fill it to overflowing with boiling water, wiping the bottom of the cup on a wet sponge.

As you turn to put the pot back on the grimy stove, you see

Woody through the corner of your eye lick his finger and stick it in the sugar bowl, sucking off the white powder with a smirk at his big sister.

"Did you get my binoculars, Dad?" he says.

"I got 'em."

"What about my mitt?"

"That too."

"What about—"

"Go see!" you laugh, finally. "All your stuff is already in your room."

Woody kicks out the chair and lopes off, jumping over a plastic laundry basket in the middle of the cluttered living room floor. "Jesus, something's gotten into him," you say to Sarah as if you were old friends. "Of course I'm thankful, but I wish I knew what happened. It seems he doesn't think about her all the time now, and I don't think he's crying himself to sleep anymore."

"I don't know either," Sarah says, biting a cuticle on her pinky, "but I gotta tell you, it is nice not to hear that boy whimpering through the wall every night. There were times over the winter," she says, looking out the living room window, "I thought he'd drive me stark raving mad." She spits out the dead skin. "I think it's Covington Parker; he spends a lot of time over there now, and his mother babies both of them like anything—ice cream, cookies, games—sometimes I think she even favors Woody."

Glancing quickly over at Michael and then back your way, she says, "I guess it must have been pretty weird back there."

But all you can manage is a weary "I'll tell you sometime."

"Listen, Dad," she says, changing her position in the chair. "I'm not gonna be able to go out with you all tonight. Buddy and I—we got plans to go up to Nags Head. I'm sorry."

"Oh, Sarah, no, not tonight," you say. "It's time for us to be together. We've got some money for the first time in more than a year.

Come on, let's celebrate. Buddy can wait; you can see him every other night of the week."

She runs her fingers through her long hair as Brenda might have done and looks over to Michael for support. He has just picked up a pack of old cards from the empty chair at the other end of the table and is laying out a game of solitaire. "Well, I'm sorry Dad, I—"

"I don't want your apologies, sweetheart, I just want you to come with the family. I mean, what are you going to do in September?" Your voice is too high, but you can't stop yourself. "Chapel Hill's a long way off and Buddy's not going to be there to fill up your calendar."

"Well, listen Dad, I know it probably isn't the right time to get into this—"

"What isn't?"

"Well, I . . . I don't think I'm gonna go."

"Where?"

"To Chapel Hill. I don't wanna go. I don't think I'm ready."

You smile, relieved for a moment. "Oh of course you are! That's ridiculous. You're gonna love it." You reach across the table and take her hand. "Your mother and I had a great time—really, some of the best times of my life." It's a harmless lie, you figure.

But she shakes her head. "I'm just not ready to go so far away. I just read something somewhere about the extension up in Elizabeth City. I think I'll do that first," she says, her voice lifting an octave at the end of the sentence. "I'm not going." She withdraws her hand.

You can feel your smile grow flat. "Of course you're going."

"No, you're not listening to me: I am not going." She takes a deep tremulous breath. "Listen, Dad, Buddy's just got a year left of school and we talked it up and down last week and—"

"And what?"

Her eyes narrow. "We, well I, thought that maybe I'd stay around here for another year; you still need help with the house and the paper. And then I'd go next year—and maybe Buddy'll join me there."

You can't stop yourself from wincing. "That's just asinine, Sarah. How could you pass up such a great opportunity? I mean they're even paying for it! Jesus, Sarah. Buddy's never going to go to college—and certainly not to UNC. He's barely literate from what I can figure," you say, instantly sorry as Sarah wipes away a tear with the tips of her long fingers.

"You know, you can be a real shit when you want to."

She's never talked to you like that and you stand because you don't know what else to do, upsetting the table with your thighs, and Michael scoops up the cards and walks away from the table.

"Where are you going?"

"Not here."

"Just wait a moment," you yelp, but Michael is already at the screen door and flipping it closed behind him. "Get back here!" you growl at the closed door, then mutter, "Y'know that little SOB's—"

"Don't call him names," Sarah blurts out.

Scolded, you lower your voice. "He's gonna be the death of me, Sarah."

"Well, he's a good person, you know. He just doesn't like school." She shows a face full of tears. "And he loves me and he'll never leave me!"

"Oh," you say, catching on.

"God, you're so snotty, Dad. I don't call Jessica names, even though she's the joke of the whole damn school!" She looks up to see your expression, but you can't breathe. "Yeah, everyone saw her comin' on to you; they all call her Horny Widow Walsh. What a joke! I don't even know how she could go on teaching there."

"You know, nothing is going on between us," you lie.

"I really don't care," she says. "Just don't go around calling Buddy names."

So you swallow, and swallow again, afraid you might say something else you'll regret; afraid that she might leave like her mother. "Listen, Sarah, honey. I wasn't talking about Buddy—it was Michael. I'm sorry." She looks up. "I'm just worried. I've had a couple of hard days. You can understand that." She exhales. "And I'm just worried that you're gonna mess up your life waiting around for Buddy. I really think he's all right, but I just don't—"

"I'm leaving," she mutters, getting up from the table. "This is getting no place."

"Please, Sarah. It's just that you're so bright."

"And what? Buddy's an idiot?"

"No, I didn't say that. You know me; it takes me a while." You force a smile. "He seems okay. You're just so different from each other. You know what I'm talking about. You're gonna go places, and Buddy, well, he's gonna stay here." You reach for her hand but she buries her hands in her armpits.

"Wake up, Dad, this is 1973. There's no place to go, and there's nothing important except loving someone and staying by their side."

For a second you hope she is joking. "Staying by their side? Jesus, Sarah, you're not joking, are you?"

She doesn't understand. And before you can stop yourself one more time, you say, "You've been listening to too much Tammy Wynette and whatshername?"

"I don't listen to Tammy whatever," she sneers, "I'm goin'."

But when she turns, you both see Woody in the hall with a mitt in his left hand and the binoculars around his neck.

"Hey bud," you say quickly, "you look great! Listen, Sarah and I are just talking about college." Woody looks her way. "Why don't you just go on over to Covington's for a little while? We're not going to leave for an hour or two." But Woody just stands there, a photograph of dread.

"It's okay, Woody," Sarah says finally. "Really."

"I know it is," he says, suddenly sounding more like Michael than anyone else in the family. "I'm going to Covington's."

As soon as you hear him go down the wooden steps, you move closer to Sarah and put your hand on her thin shoulder. "Let's not fight. Why don't you come along? We can talk over dinner."

But she walks away, your hand sliding down her upper arm. "Jesus, Dad, you just don't get it. I don't even know where you're at anymore. I am not going tonight and I'm not going to Chapel Hill next month." She picks up her purse from the coffee table.

A moment later her hand is on the doorknob and she is walking out the door.

* * *

Two hours later, Jessica's eyes are dashing around the scattered group of diners at Evan's Crab House. "I'm serious, Jess. I can't believe some of the things I've said since Brenda . . ." You still don't know whether to say left or died.

"Well," she says, maybe too quickly, "I guess you didn't know yourself very well, did you?"

"What are you doing?" you whisper. "I thought you were the one who understood . . . the only one."

She rips open a jimmie, exposing its gray lungs and white cavities of meat. "You think you're so damn special, Peter, that no one knows your pain. That's why you're eating alone tonight."

You look around uselessly at the empty table. Woody had decided to eat Mrs. Parker's pot roast, and Michael and Sarah have never returned.

And just as suddenly, Jessica must sense that she has stepped over some line you've drawn in the sand and has to retreat. "Hey," she says softly, "don't mind me. Rough day." She drops her lower lip cutely and reaches for your arm.

* * *

A week later while you stand together out on the top deck, you mumble something inarticulate and throw a wet towel down to the sand twenty feet below. "Last night she told me that she and that little punk want to get married." You look over to check her reaction, but she's staring out at the leaning sea oats. "I think she just said it to get to me, but I just went crazy, screaming and yelling, threatening . . ." Your voice trails off. "Then," you say in a hoarse whisper, "goddamn Michael told me to settle down .. me! . . . and the next thing I knew I was screaming at him to get out of my sight!"

Jessica doesn't turn her head, and when she doesn't say anything, lost in some memory that is not yours, you just go on: "He didn't come home last night. I waited up all night. I don't know Jessica . . . I don't know what I'm doing anymore. How could she do that to me?"

"You?"

"Yeah, me."

"You know, it's not just about you." That had been Brenda's most effective line when you two fought, leaving you speechless, clogged, struggling for air, desperately turning for a way out. You are near the steps when she calls out, "Go ahead, leave!"

"I'm not the one who left!" you yell back.

"What are you doing, Peter? I'm the only one left who will listen to your crap anymore! Listen to yourself for once."

You turn halfway down the wobbly steps, one foot lower than the other, and your rage whisks off in the breezy air. "Lay off, Jessica. I'm no high school kid who needs your TV psychology. I'm lost. Don't you see?"

Now she looks like she has been slapped. "Well, let's just talk, Peter."

You squint, looking up at her watery eyes. "There's nothing to talk about. I guess it just has to pass. I'm sorry."

She nods. "Listen, I saw Michael this afternoon over at the school playing basketball.He seemed all right. And, just for the record, Buddy's not such a bad kid—I had him all year in class—and, if little else, he really does seem to care about Sarah."

"So do I."

"And so do I."

So you shift your weight and walk back up the stairs to take her outstretched hand. She pulls you close, gets up on her tiptoes. "So, just shut up about the little punk and let's watch the sunset."

Woody comes bounding up both sets of stairs, breathlessly chewing gum and asking about dinner. The words are no sooner out of his parched lips than he notices the two hands intertwined.

You try to pull away, but Jessica squeezes tighter. So you motion Woody over to the other side of your body and put your arm around the frail boy's shoulder.

Although you had intended to watch the sunset, the three of you end up leaning on the front rail looking out over the round dunes toward the deep blue ocean, calm and almost quiet, your backs toward the orange and pink glow shimmering across Pamlico Sound. No one says a word, watching a group of renters walk back across the sands to the gray beachbox across the road.

And as soon as they disappear inside the rental, a battered and rusted white VW beetle rolls slowly down the road and passes in front of the cottage.

"I like those," Jessica says.

"So did Brenda," you say without thinking, rubbing Woody's bare elbow. "They're the most ridiculous things, though . . ." You look at your watch then and pat the boy on his bony hip. "Hey, Woody, go get ready for dinner; maybe we'll go up to Nags Head for a movie tonight."

Holding your breath until you hear Woody walking across the lower deck, you turn and hug Jessica, her supple breasts pressed to your chest. And for the first time in seventeen months you long to be with a woman other than the memory of Brenda Hudson.

Chapter 8

Hatteras Island, Fall 1973

GIVING THANKS

The weeks after Labor Day are the most beautiful on Hatteras Island. The throngs of tourists are gone, the weather is warm and summery and the fishing is bountiful. September is the time when we who live on the island begin to relax again, get in touch with old friends, count the receipts from the summer and begin preparation for the fall hunting and fishing seasons. It is a time when we all thank God for the small piece of paradise that we have found down here.

—The Editor

You agonize over that last line before making it the lead editorial (on top of some more substantive pieces about offshore drilling and the dredging of Oregon Inlet) in the September 10th First Anniversary Edition of *The Island Weekly*. What a pile of crap, you think as you jam the period key with your index finger and then lean back in the wobbly kitchen chair, wondering if you somehow hadn't really come to believe every word of it.

And after another sip of lukewarm Folgers, you are thinking of postponing a pretty good feature about September being the heart of hurricane season. It might not be upbeat enough for an anniversary edition.

Over the past year *The Island Weekly* had become more successful than anyone would have imagined, in part because you apparently had a knack for anticipating what tourists and locals alike wanted to read—and in part, as well, because you were being slowly transformed, typewriter ribbon by typewriter ribbon, weekly edition by weekly edition, into the kind of slightly disheveled community voice you might have once scorned back in the Rosslyn days.

The paper had even started gaining out-of-town subscribers—most likely cottage owners, though there was no way then to track them. On the good days you and Sarah had shared a running joke about the five families from some small town in upstate New York—Elting—the Lewises, the Cilibertos, the Domitrovits, the Tevises, and the Hills—and some other odd ones from Colorado, New Mexico, Florida, and maybe a dozen scattered around Ohio. A couple of first name initials whose gender you debated on cold windy nights . . . M. Shire from New Orleans who changed addresses three times, last one Milwaukee; a J. Pedro from Milford, CT; a J. Trapani from Northampton, MA.

You are not unaware or unappreciative, though, of the role that Sarah played in that remarkable change. From that first crude eight-page edition of the *Weekly*, she had served as the official "shit censor" for you, who, in your early zeal to sell more and more newspapers, often overdid the good ol' boy routine in your editorials. She would groan and grimace from across the cluttered, paper-strewn coffee table, clasping her stomach and falling sideways on the couch—or stick a finger down her throat every time you'd read aloud an editorial passage that absolutely reeked of patronizing sentimentality.

During the first few months of the operation you suspected she may have done it to protect you and her siblings from the hostile backlash she knew was possible from the normally suspicious Islanders, who would shun you if they felt they were being mocked;

she continued it later, even as your voice lost the huckster's phony twang, because she felt increasingly embarrassed in direct proportion to her involvement with Buddy Neuse. Which was growing by the day.

By September, however, she is effectively no longer around to save you from yourself. "If it hadn't been for you, this paper would have been fish wrap," you sputter a few mornings after writing the cheesy editorial, tossing a heavy stack of papers to the dirty floor. The whole cottage shakes. You are hoping beyond reasonable hope that she will come with you to the Ocracoke Ferry to deliver a load of the anniversary edition, but her hand is already on the loose knob. In a moment you feel her footsteps on the wooden stairs.

The two of you have hardly spoken in a month. Despite your undisguised wishes, Sarah had not gone to Chapel Hill near the end of August, but had stayed on the island to be around Buddy. She still sleeps and eats at the cottage, continues to write her columns, and grimly assists with the pasteup. But practically every other waking hour is spent with Buddy Neuse, hanging out over at Richie's Texaco at the sullen and empty edge of Rodanthe, making out in the back seat of his primered GTO convertible, and, later, shutting off the lights and sneaking off to their secret spot, Buddy's late grandmother's abandoned trailer down in Salvo.

Sarah no longer has any desire to help, only to do her job like any employee waiting for the whistle to blow and to get out. For good. To please you, or more to the point, to get you off her back, she had signed up for a University of North Carolina Freshman Composition course at the extension in Elizabeth City, and had even driven up there on lonely Route 17 in the van for the first two classes of "endless boring hours with half-wits and a pinched-nosed recovering librarian."

Months later, though, in the blustery middle of October, when, mostly out of boredom, you ask about her grades, she says, "I walked out of the fifth or sixth class during the ten-minute break thinking I was going to suffocate—and never returned." She looks at you with that smirk you had once loved. "I never even went back for the argumentative essay I wrote about the refund I deserved."

* * *

"Y'know, the trouble began when she started going out with that little turd," you mutter to Jessica, who has taken over some of Sarah's responsibilities. And the trouble resurfaces, like a fin along the shore, when Sarah stands right in front of you, hands on hips, and says she isn't ever going to Chapel Hill. "For the second semester—or any other stinking time! I don't ever want to go to that goddamn snotty place!"

You shake your head and turn away to hide the pooling in your eyes. And figuring you deserve better than the insolent brat that stands so brazenly in front of you, you mutter, "I don't give a damn what you do, Sarah. You want to ruin your life, go right ahead."

"I don't know what I was thinking," you tell Jessica later. "I guess I was expecting that she'd be so shocked at my giving up that she'd cry a flood of tears that I might soak up on my shoulder." Jessica shakes her head. "But there she was chewing on the inside of her cheek and glaring dry-eyed at me as if I were the most contemptible piece of shit on the face of the earth."

* * *

A few weeks later on, flustered and desperate to get the week's copy to the printers before deadline, you go searching for a blue editing pencil in various drawers and under cushions, eventually rummaging through the pocketbook Sarah has left on the couch.

When you grab ahold of a round dispenser of pills, you are

instantly carried off, as if in another riptide, to the center of some rage you had first come to recognize in yourself when Brenda turned the corner on the morning she left.

"What the hell is this!" you say, knocking the bedroom door against the wall and shaking the dispenser in the air. Sarah is lying on the bed writing a piece about the Hoopers' fiftieth anniversary party as you stand over her, holding the dispenser inches from her nose.

She leans back to the wall, her chin tucked into her throat. "What the hell were you doing in my stuff?"

"It doesn't matter what I was doing there!" Your voice is an octave too high and already way beyond your control. "It's bad enough that you go out with him, but to go to bed with him . . . what the hell is wrong with you, Sarah?"

"It's none of your damn business!" she says, grabbing at your outstretched hand and trying to claw at the dispenser. "Give it to me! It's mine!"

But you jerk it back and wrap your shaking fist around it, holding it up in the air as some kind of prize, and then, turning sharply, stomp into the bathroom where you rip the plastic lid off the dispenser, your hands shaking as you spill the small pills into the bowl, two or three skidding off the toilet seat and across the buckled linoleum floor.

Still trembling from the inside out you walk back across the narrow hall and find her lying face down on the unmade bed, the feather pillow muffling her sobs. "I don't ever want to see him around again!" you scream. "I've taken enough shit to bury nine people and I just won't take any more." You poke hard at her back with a rigid finger. "Do you hear me?!"

She doesn't move, her back expanding and contracting, expanding and contracting, her face buried in the pillow, her hands cupping her ears. So you fling the splintery plastic remains of the dispenser at the torn screen behind her head. "Sarah!"

But she will not stir, the only movement her ribs expanding and contracting. Rising and falling. Up and down. Air rushes through your nostrils. And before a single reasoned thought is able to wriggle out of your consciousness, you have your shaking hands on her slight hips and have picked her up as one does a small child, swinging her gangly form over your knees and smacking her with an open hand on her thin cotton shorts.

* * *

An hour or two later, you look up from the typewriter on the Formica table as Sarah whisks by and stomps out the screen door, the slap of wood on wood coming a few seconds after she disappears. And when Jessica, who's been sitting with her since the explosion, follows in her wake a few moments later, you ask, "Where's she going?" pointing out at the empty deck.

"I don't know," she says, pursing her lips. "With Buddy."

You drop your head. "I did it again, Jessica."

She nods, turning away. "She told me all about it. She thinks you're crazy."

"I'm sorry. You know. You know. I know you know. I just lost the handle when I saw those pills. It was just too much—"

"Well, tell that to Sarah," she says, grabbing her purse. "I'm tired. I'm goin' home. You're gonna lose everybody if you don't watch it, Peter. This is getting old."

Then she opens the screen door and swings it behind her so hard it bounces open again.

Chapter 9

So you sit there, deserted by everyone, torturing yourself with visions of Sarah jumping into the rumbling GTO, taking Buddy's thin, ugly, pimply face in her hands and pushing her open mouth gently against his.

And hours later, while it turns out Buddy and Sarah are down in Salvo, drinking beer after beer on the slanted deck outside his grandmother's rusted old trailer, the air cool and moist, full of the honking of frogs and scratching of crickets, the faint rumble of the waves way out in the darkness, you are leaning over the lower deck railing in Rodanthe looking down the empty road, waiting for your daughter's return.

You are descending, as you've descended so many times before, into what is now a grainy rerun of how different everything would have been if Brenda had just come back that day. You didn't ask for this. You didn't do anything to deserve it. You imagine yourself as Job caught in the middle of some cosmic bet to test your faith. You know in your heart that you are being punished for something you did not do. Even so, you're willing to repent. "Just tell me what I've done!" you wail.

But there is nothing you can do to make things right. So you wait until 3:30 to call Jessica, who hasn't heard from her, and Mrs. Neuse, who is drunk, and the hospital in Elizabeth City, which has no record of a Sarah Hudson being admitted, and finally wake up Bruce Hill, the Dare County Sheriff, just like you did when Brenda disappeared.

"Pete, settle down. They're probably out with their friends—up to no good, but, y'know, okay. Now, take my advice and go back to sleep. You'll find 'er and paddle 'er in the mornin'."

"They're three hours late, Bruce. She's never late. We had words . . . and now she's out with that little sonofabitch!"

"Watch it, Pete," he quickly cuts you off. "He's my wife's nephew, remember."

"Right now I don't give a shit. I can't go through this again. What the hell can I do?"

Bruce always has an answer. "Pour yourself one inch of bourbon and go back to sleep. I'll check around and call you in the mornin'."

And now there really is nothing to do but take his advice; you go over to the table and pour yourself two fingers of Jim Beam and pace anxiously back and forth across the small living room, walking out and staring across the empty sands and then walking in again, only to walk out one more time, just as you've done hundreds of times over the past year and a half.

Suddenly there is a rustling on the upper deck. "Thank God!" you stutter, and lope up the shaking steps, bending down and shaking the curled form in the sleeping bag. "I'm really sorry, Sarah . . ."

But it's Michael who lifts his groggy head out of the sleeping bag. "What the hell . . . ?"

"Who is that?"

"Who the hell do you think it is?"

"Oh Jesus, Michael, it's you. I thought . . . well, it doesn't matter what I think." You step over the bag and look out over the dark dunes. "Michael, will you take the van and go look for your sister? She's not here."

Michael looks at you like you're crazy. "She'll come home." He lays his head back down on his arm. "I gotta get some sleep—I'm goin' to that clinic up in Chapel Hill tomorrow."

"What clinic?"

"The one the coach is taking me to. We're leavin' at six."

"Well that doesn't matter right now. I want you to go find your sister."

"But I—"

"Go, dammit!" you growl out across the empty beach, pointing to nothing in particular.

You don't know what he'll do, but are surprised when he forces himself out of the sleeping bag muttering that he knows why she left.

Just then some lights pierce the darkness near the hotel and head your way.

"There she is," he says. "I'm going back to sleep."

You don't say anything, your heart pounding against the inside of your aching chest. As the car approaches the cottage, you realize it isn't the sound of Buddy's big Pontiac engine. It's Jessica.

"That woman's gonna make me believe in God again," you say not unhappily.

"What?"

"Nothing. Please just take the van and go find your sister."

Michael takes a deep breath that he doesn't expel until he has stepped into his flip-flops and passes Jessica racing up the steps, avoiding her glance as he usually does, head down, waving awkwardly.

"Where ya goin'?"

"He sent me to look for Sarah . . ." His deep voice trails off as he continues down the steps.

Jessica is out of breath when she gets up on the deck, taking your hand from the railing and squeezing. "Where's he goin'?"

"Just to look; he probably knows their spots better than I would," you say. "I just pray they haven't run off."

She lifts your hand to her cheek. "Thanks for coming, Jessica," you murmur. "I'm a basket case. And you're too good to me."

"Well, I probably am—but that's my fault, right? Let's go down and get some coffee."

And by the time you sit down in the beaten rockers on the lower deck with the hot coffee, the sun is rising up over the dunes, the sky as warm and orange as it was ever supposed to be, and still nothing is right in your life.

* * *

When Michael returns at 6:45, just in time to meet the coach, who waves out the van window from the road, you despair of ever seeing your daughter again. And the worst of it, you think, now looking over at Jessica, is that you already know what it's going to feel like, and how it will never go away.

At 7:30, you hear Woody stirring down in the cottage and then turn mechanically at the familiar hum of Buddy's GTO. It stops way down on the road, the engine rumbling like a stalled tornado.

From your perch on the upper deck you can just make out Sarah giving Buddy a long, passionate kiss and then walking head down along the edge of the quiet road and over to the cottage. You can hear her pulling herself up each step by holding on to the rail. Then the screen door open and clap shut.

You say nothing. There is nothing to say, turning and taking Jessica in your arms and kissing her as passionately and gratefully as your daughter had just done to Buddy.

"Come to my house," she whispers, and you bury your eyes in her shoulder.

A few moments later, you take her shoulders in your hands, push yourself back and say, "I can't, Jessica. I just can't. Not yet."

Chapter 10

You are alone, again, sitting at the kitchen table, a coffee cup in your hand, reading an old *Time* magazine, waiting for your daughter to come home. Woody is at Covington's house. You have no idea where Michael might be.

You hear a car pull in, a door slam, another door slam. You hold your breath, expecting Sarah and Buddy to walk in.

You are surprised, though, to see Jessica standing in the doorway. "Sarah wants to tell you something," is all she says and then steps aside. Your wide-eyed daughter walks slowly into the living room, looking like a five-year-old waiting for her daddy to explode.

You think you know what is coming. But five agonizing, teary minutes later you put the coffee cup down on the table and begin weeping at the startling news, first your lower lip trembling and then your eyes flooding, spilling over as you turn away, dropping your face into the cup of your palms.

Your daughter reaches across the messy table to touch the top of your balding head, but you can see that she pulls back as you lift your splotchy face.

"I'm sorry, Daddy."

You shake your head. "No. I'm so sorry, baby," you say. "This is all my fault, isn't it?"

She doesn't answer, just smiles so sadly that you think you might begin to wail, walks around the rectangular table, long fingers barely touching the sticky yellow surface as she makes the circuit and sits in your lap, turns her soft cheek onto your warm shoulder, and weeps.

* * *

Later that evening, after Sarah wanders out to walk the beach, Jessica pours two jelly glasses of Beam and water, hands one to you, and then sits down on the pilly couch, takes a sip, puts it down, and leans against your shoulder.

And when it becomes clear that you aren't going to say anything, that you can't say anything, she begins to tell you about her long day in the car with Sarah . . . and some of what you don't know about the much longer days before:

She tells you how Sarah had figured that the queasiness that came every early morning was nothing more than the result of having to live with an angry, bereft father. Some mornings she wondered whether the nausea was somehow connected to the lying about going to classes up in Elizabeth City.

But by the approach of Halloween, when she was vomiting every early morning, she finally understood. "She told me she wanted to stop every woman she passed in the aisles at the Avon Grocery or the Community Center down in Hatteras Village—the ones who looked like mothers—and ask if what she was feeling was okay. She said she lay in bed those fall evenings longing to curl up with her mother on the king-sized bed back in Rosslyn and cry and laugh like two women on TV sharing something only they can know."

And with the empty glass in your hand, resting on your knee, you stare ahead at Jessica's full glass of bourbon on the table, yearning to lean over and reach it, but instead go on listening.

Listening to how Buddy, now a senior at the Cape Hatteras School, is being courted by Tina Midgett, Laura O'Neal, and Charles Willett, United States Army recruiter. Which is to say he is not nearly as available as he had been in the warm weather.

Jessica sits up then, reaches for the jelly glass and downs the rest of the bourbon. "I've been teaching Island seniors long enough to know," she says, "that Buddy figured everything good about living was right out in front of him—and it would only last a very short time. He'd already seen hundreds of times—mornings on the docks, nights at the bars—the despair that comes from waking up one morning and realizing his youth was gone, misspent . . . and there'd be nothing much ahead but toil until he was dead."

Buddy insisted, finally, that after Thanksgiving, when the last of the tourist fishermen would leave the boarded up island, she had to go up to Elizabeth City and have an abortion.

Mincing no words, Jessica tells you exactly what Sarah had told her, how the two of them had driven over to the Salvo trailer, fooled around, and had some cigarettes and beer. Then Buddy told her he had enlisted in the Marines and would be leaving for Parris Island right after school ended in June.

And as she talks on and on, you lose track of her voice and begin filling in the details like you're in a movie, like you're not even there:

FAde In: Salvo, NC

[Sarah and Buddy]

[At Buddy's grandmother's trailer]

[Sarah]

What do you wanna do that for, Buddy? You don't have to go in.

[BUDDY]

I'm goin' in, Suds. What the hell am I gonna do here?—get stuck on this stinkin' island for the res' of my life?

[SARAH]

We'll be out of here by July. We'll be on our way to L.A. together, like we dreamed about . . . a pink bungalow, a job doing promotion on the MGM lot, everything chartreuse and new and clean. Remember?

[BUDDY]

Listen, I got $350. That's what it costs up in Norfolk. We could drive up there one mornin' and be back 'fore dinner. It'll be easy.

Nobody'll know."

[SARAH]

Where'd you get $350?

[BUDDY]

Don't matter. I got it and that's what it'll cost. I already called in. We can make an appointment on Monday and go in on Wednesday and have 'er done.

[Buddy lights a Marlboro and takes a long drag—and holds it.]

[SARAH]

Buddy, I don't think I can do that.

[Buddy stuffs the cash in his front pocket and goes over to the mattress.]

[BUDDY]

Course you can, Suds. Course you can. It's safe. Debbie John had one done up there, that's how I found out about'er. Jamey told me."

[Sarah shakes her head and pulls the quilt up under her chin. Buddy flicks an ash onto the floor.]

[SARAH]

It'll be all right, Buddy—we'll work it out. We'll get out of here in June and head straight for L.A.

[BUDDY]

It ain't gonna work.

[SARAH]

Yeah, baby . . . I know what you—

[BUDDY]

No! I ain't gonna do it! Not for you. Not fer no one. I ain't gonna ruin my life. Not now.

[SARAH]

But what am I gonna do?

[BUDDY]

I'll tell you what you're gonna do, girl: you're gonna go up there and have it done!

[SARAH]

I can't . . .

[BUDDY]

Well, fuckit, neither can't I, Suds, I just can't do it now.

[SARAH]

But Buddy, I already started to think about it like it was ours. It is ours.

[BUDDY]

It ain't mine. You told me that you were on the goddamn pill. I didn't ask for this, and I ain't gonna have it. And I ain't gonna marry you, not for nothin'. I'll drive you all the way the hell up there and I'll goddamn pay for it, but I ain't gonna marry you.

[SARAH]

Get out of here! Get out of here.

[BUDDY]

Don't you go 'n' tell no one that I didn't offern to take care of it fer you.

[SARAH]

GET OUT OF HERE!!

* * *

When you realize that everything has gone silent, you look up and see Jessica at the sink dribbling some water into the jelly glasses.

Holding the glasses out like candles, she tells you that by the time Sarah made it to Jessica's cottage, the sun had disappeared behind Pamlico Sound. She banged on the wooden frame of the screen door and let her puffy face and wild hair speak for her as she stood helplessly, hands at her sides, out on the sloping porch. "I reached out to pull that forlorn girl into my arms and she laid her cheek on my shoulder and sobbed and sobbed and sobbed and then suddenly looked up and grew stiff."

And so Jessica tells you about Carl Jesskins, Mr. Jesskins, the other English teacher down at the school. Your mouth goes dry, but you are too wrung out to do anything but take a gulp of the bourbon.

You hear that Jesskins was holding two wine glasses when Sarah pushed herself away and ran out the door, off the porch into the windy darkness. You get the picture. You don't need the explanation.

But she tells you anyway—and you can't stop her. Like a riptide carrying you farther and farther away from the beach, you know you should change the subject, swim sideways out of it, but you're too tired, too weak, and just let the current carry you out.

You lean back on the couch, hands cupped around the nearly empty jelly glass, as Jessica tells you how she had practically begged Sarah to come along with her to Raleigh for the day—to visit her grandfather, to pick weeds and plant flowers at her husband's grave, to explain to the bereaved girl what Carl Jesskins was doing at her cottage the night before.

"She didn't say a word until we crossed Croatan Sound and were a mile or two into Mann's Harbor, and then she burst out, 'How could you?'

" 'How could I do what?' I snapped back. I wasn't going to let her make me feel guilty.

"But then I felt guilty and started to try to explain how things were between you and me."

You turn your head at that and look over Jessica. Her beautiful sculpted face. She is expressionless, just a hard stare waiting for your eyes to find hers.

Then she begins: "Sarah said, 'I thought you liked my father.' She was chewing on her lower lip.

" 'I do,' I said. I told her I love you, but you won't let me. I told her that you're still walking the beach looking for her mother.

"So she says, 'That's why he needs you so much. How could you cheat on him like that?' "

You see Jessica smile at the childish assumption you both understand without need for explanation. And when the smile disappears, she tells you how she explained to Sarah that she would only be cheating if there was a relationship. "I told her, 'I'm really just the woman who bandages his wounds.' "

That hurt. That hurt so much that you close your eyes and lean back and let the current of Jessica's monotone take you farther from the shore. You hear something about Scuppernog, and then how the two of them drove into a Bob's Big Boy in downtown Rocky Mount full of the after-church crowd.

Jessica is then wondering aloud where Jesus had gone in her life. She's left you behind and is speaking into the stagnant cottage air about the stiff feel of the white confirmation dress, the way her mother looked at her standing in front of the cheval mirror.

And when you pick up the thread again, it's an hour and a half later in Jessica's flat narrative and the two of them are in the parking lot of the Wake County Nursing Home. "It was cool out; leaves were drifting across the parking lot. I told Sarah in the elevator that he wouldn't recognize me.

"The hall smelled of Lysol. I took Sarah's hand and we walked into the small light-green room with two beds. One bed was empty. My grampa," she says, pausing and smiling at something that doesn't involve you, "looked as much like a plucked chicken as a person staring off at nothing. He didn't move, not even when I took his hand off the sheet."

Now she smiles, but not at you. "Sarah was practically catatonic."

Then the smile disappears again. "On the way out of the room—we couldn't have been in there more than two minutes—Sarah finally found her voice. She wanted to know how long he'd been like that.

"I told her, 'Years.' Told her I just show up every once in a while to make sure he's being treated okay. Told her my Meemaw died in '65, I think, and he just sort of disintegrated after that."

You realize that you don't know any of that.

"Then she wanted to know about my parents. So I told her that they moved to Sarasota in Florida after I graduated from high school. And then . . . well, then I drove off and took her to see my high school.

"Sarah said it looked just like her high school in Rosslyn." She pauses then and you turn your head to see if she's looking at you, but she's staring ahead as if she's in a trance. "I drove past the open chain-link gates and then all around the empty parking lot covered with pine needles, pointing out all the private memories that I could tell an eighteen-year-old.

"Her eyes were pooling so I asked what she was thinking really. She shook her head and said, 'Just my old friends. They're all in college right now. I'm not even sure I'd like them all anymore. But I am sure that the whole group back at RHS would find the whole thing with Buddy totally repulsive.'

"Then we went to the Wake County Cemetery. It's a massive place with thousands of grave markers and trees and roads as far as you can see. I could feel Sarah's eyes on me as I pulled off to the side, took a deep breath, let it out very slowly, killed the engine, and got out. Sarah stayed in the car as I walked over to a small marker. I knelt down, crossed myself like I always do, and touched the cool stone."

You are picturing the whole scene when you realize that Jessica has taken out of her pocket a curling black-and-white photograph of a gravestone and is holding it in front of your face.

Robert W. Walsh
August 10, 1944–October 29, 1968
"The Good Die Young"

"So I did what I did, what I always do, then I looked and saw Sarah still sitting in the car, wiping her eyes with the tissues from the pack that I had handed her over an hour or two before. It was time to go. She didn't even turn her head when I slid back into the driver's seat and pulled the door shut.

" 'Vietnam?' Sarah asked me, but I couldn't speak just then."

Then she turns to you, shakes her head, speaks to you for the first time in what might have been hours. "No. He just got drunk and had an accident the week before he was to ship out."

* * *

You open your arms to Jessica Walsh with the tenderest feelings of love and lust and earthly gratitude that anyone knows.

"Sloppy love . . . Slove," you call it with a silly giggle as the two of you lie in bed hours later in her sound-side cottage. "Look at me, I'm laughing," you chortle. "I'm so stupid . . . look at me!"

And long after Jessica falls asleep in your arms, you lie awake staring through the breezy window at the star-filled sky, feeling so curiously alive and joyful and hopeless, all at the same time.

Being with Jessica after so much time alone with the memory of Brenda is perhaps even more wonderful than any of the desperate fantasies you had sometimes barely allowed yourself in the anxious minutes before badgering yourself out of bed each lonely morning to go run the empty beach. Jessica was seductive, inviting, all tongue and fingertips, her breath an urgent breeze along your tingling skin.

And even after Jessica slips into that sweet glow of sleep after love, her ear in the hollow of your shoulder when the bloodhounds begin howling outside the fluttering screen as you knew they surely would—you are for this moment alone simply happy to be right where you are, the sea smell of her hair filling your mind.

You breathe in deeply and, looking through the moonlight at her blond hair spilling over her perfectly curved cheeks and onto your bare chest, her round hip under the white sheet, you see yourself slipping out of bed, tiptoeing out of the cottage, driving back to Rodanthe, sprinting across the scrub grasses scratching at your calves, long needled cacti biting the tender soles of your feet before you break free, racing through waving sea oats and over the tall dune to the sea, diving headlong through the crashing waves, feet kicking, arms swinging until you are past the break, the tide moving you farther and farther out, past the pier, past the wreck, shallow breaths, shallow breaths are all you can do to keep from panicking, another woman with a power to move you beyond your will, beyond the intention of your life, the tide pulling you farther and farther out, and you see yourself at the altar, the first of an endless hold-your-breath concessions and corrections until your life is again no longer your own, as indistinguishable as the flotsam from the current along which it is carried . . . a baby floating by, then a house, and then what? . . . nothing to do to keep from disappearing off the edge of the horizon, the arc of heaven and earth, but to swim sideways, stroke after stroke after stroke until you lean back and feel the current moving you back to shore.

And with only the muffled surf lapping at the reedy shore of the sound, curtains fluttering, you turn and gently press your lips onto Jessica's creamy shoulder and then the soft skin just below her chin, the girl's chest between the woman's warm breasts, easing yourself down to lay a rough cheek on the brown softness of her sleeping belly, your ear pressed to her hip bone. When she wakes, her fingers holding on to your jawbone, coaxing your mouth all the way up to hers, now moving under you like the warm ocean, the last ounce of resistance leaves from your arching aching body.

You sleep late into the morning, the first daybreak in more than eight hundred daybreaks on the island since Brenda disappeared that you won't run the beach.

Chapter 11

Rodanthe, Summer 1974

Later on, you piece together the stories Sarah and Woody tell about what happened before you got home:

Sarah pivots to see who is opening the screen door, and suddenly her shorts and legs are wet, a puddle disappearing into the carpet.

Stumbling through the doorway, Woody hears her gasp, sees the dark splotches on her maternity shorts, and drops his jaw, eyes twinkling as his big sister just stands there, palms up as if someone is pointing at her.

It takes her more than a few seconds to understand that her water has broken. But in the briefest of meantimes, as she tells Jessica later—and Jessica tells you—Woody has scooted into the cottage and did a backflip onto the couch, laughing and pointing, one leg way up in the air. "Sarah peed her pants! Sarah peed her pants!"

"Shut up, you fool!" she cries, a crow's cawing in her thin voice, trying to grasp her body's apparent miscalculation. It is weeks too early to go into labor and, besides, it isn't anything like Mrs. Parker and Mrs. Hill said it would be. She looks all around. Someone has to call Maude Aycock. Someone has to get Jessica.

But all Woody can see is her wet shorts and the splotch on the rug. No one had thought to tell him about those things; he still spends all his time up the road at Covington Parker's brick house. A burst of mucus rolls over his lips when he can no longer hold his breath.

"I said shut up, Woody!" she says, bending over and pushing his shoulder. "Go get Jessica. She's down at the beach . . . and tell Dad! Now! Just do something!" She is weeping, holding her little brother down on the couch even as she is yelling at him to get up. "GET. UP!"

Woody slides out from beneath his sister's clenched fingers, races out the screen door, and runs down the steps, jumping the last four and slipping in the sand. He picks himself up and sprints across the deserted road along the path you had raked out of the beach scrub all the way to the dunes, screaming at the top of his lungs long before he trudged up to the peak, "Jessicaaaaaaah! Hey, hey Jessicaaaaaaaaaaah!"

* * *

Twisting around on the blanket and leaning into your elbow, you see Woody slide down the other side of the dune to the empty beach, green and clear as when you first discovered it in 1962. Jessica is just then wading out of the foamy surf and sees Woody racing toward her, waving his arms and screaming her name.

She just stands there dripping, the life drained from her beautiful face. She looks like she sees a ghost. Or maybe Brenda Hudson.

But Woody is all alone. "Jessicaaaaaaaaah!" he screeches again and bends over on his knees to catch his breath while she stands rigid, ankle deep in the surf.

"C'mere!!" he says, waving her over to the blanket as she finally steps out of the surf and stumbles through the soft sand. "Sarah peed in her pants! Sarah peed her pants!" He laughs and jumps back from a wave. "She wants you! Right now!"

You see Jessica smile brightly, the shadows moving off her cheeks as she jogs so naturally over to the blanket, grabbing a towel and covering her face as you stare at the light curly blond hairs on her brown thighs against the black bikini. “Let’s go there, grandpa!” she says, holding out her hand and grinning as widely as Woody, who has already run back.

But you can’t move. You want to stay suspended in this moment.

“Hey, come on, gramps! Sarah’s ready to do it; her water broke . . .” She still has her hand out.

“What?”

Jessica frowns. “It’s time, wake up! We have to get back there and you have to get Maudie.”

You take her hand and suck in a deep anxious breath as she helps pull you to your feet—and then runs off toward the path through the dunes, disappearing over the other side.

* * *

When you finally get back to the cottage, Jessica is standing on the lower deck, already dressed in red shorts and a white top, a red sweatshirt in her hand. “First go give Sarah a hug,” she calls down, just like a teacher, “and then drive straight over to the Aycocks’. Tell Maudie the water’s broke and she’s had two weak contractions since then in”—she looks at her watch—”say fifteen minutes.”

Grateful that Jessica is running things, you are pleased just to follow instructions instead of having to pretend to be in control of something you know nothing about. Brenda was so private about the births, and you had asked so little, content to know nothing, to look away from all the mess of life.

So when you find Sarah in her room, standing at the window, round and flushed, wearing a long white nightshirt, she looks so much like Brenda, her eyes like a newborn colt looking at the green world for the first frightening time, your lip begins to tremble, and you lean over her massive belly and kiss her awkwardly on the cheek. Sarah grabs your arm and looks into your wet eyes. “Hey, that's supposed to happen later," she laughs.

"Oh, you know the new me," you say, wiping your cheek with your shoulder. "Just a faucet of tears."

A memory seems to darken her mottled face before she brightens again, pressing her hard belly awkwardly into your midsection and wrapping her long arms around your neck, your head floating like a kite tethered high above the deck, your chin on the top of her head.

Sarah stands on her tiptoes, pulling gently on the back of your neck and pressing her lips to your ear. "I just wish . . . Mom were here."

"I know," you say, stroking her long hair, "I know," until you feel her tighten and pull away.

Jessica is in the doorway. "Contraction?" she says brightly, and Sarah nods and wipes her eye, her fingers cupped around her tight belly.

The spasm is over in twenty seconds, and as soon as Jessica sees Sarah take a deep breath she taps you on the shoulder and tells you again to get Maude. "Tell her it was three. Tell her they're comin' every ten minutes."

On the squealing, fishtailing seventy-five-miles-per-hour three-mile drive down to Salvo, with a spark of light jumping off the shiny bumper of a car passing the other way, you feel a gust of the old cold rage sweep through your skull. For a moment you want to strangle Buddy, and then, glancing sideways to the empty blue passenger seat, feeling for a hand, a rope, anything, you shrug and, as easily as a flash of light skipping off some chrome bumper, you feel the rage fly away like a kite, the line cut as you turn into the unmarked sand drive between wide bent cedars.

Maudie's seventeen-year-old daughter answers the trailer door with a naked infant boy in her arms. "Hey Laurie, is your Ma around?" You look down at your flip-flops. "My Sarah's just starting . . . y'know, the baby . . ."

Laurie snickers at your discomfort. "Well, you jes' come on in, Mr. Hudson. I'll git Mama, she's out back—sweet tea, Mr. Hudson?"

"No, no thanks, Laurie." You are about to tell her to call you Pete like everyone else does on the island, but you let it go as she sashays heavily down the dark, narrow hall just as Maudie comes out into the stuffy living room wearing a sleeveless flowered dress. Her fat white arms almost match the background of the cloth.

"Hey there Pete, it's 'bout time, huh?" She waddles over to the messy kitchen table to get an old leather briefcase and a canvas beach bag from the Ben Franklin. "You think you're ready for this?" Her voice is slow like hot tar.

You shrug. "I got nothing to be ready for, Maudie—Sarah's gonna do it all."

"Don't bet on it." Maudie must be fifty, but she looks at least sixty-five, a nest of Brillo gray hair on top of her head and round cheeks and chin that always look red hot.

As far as you have been able to gather, driving up and down Highway 12 for the last two years, Maudie Aycock has been the island's midwife since her own mother went blind from diabetes just before the Bonner Bridge replaced the ferry as Hatteras's link to the world. And she has delivered maybe a third or a half of the kids who are at the high school right now. But over the past ten years more and more of the Island women travel up to Elizabeth City to do their birthing with a real doctor in the more modern and sterile surroundings at Memorial Hospital.

You had assumed that Sarah would take care of everything up there, but then the obstetrician, Dr. Pole, told the three of you that he had serious doubts about whether Sarah would make it up there in time. As he said to your profound discomfort, her large pelvic dimensions and her mother's history of extremely rapid birth (you wondered how the man knew that!) suggested that she might indeed do the same thing—and end up giving birth on NC Highway

168. So he suggested that Sarah should make arrangements to move up to Elizabeth City in late April and spend the last six weeks near the hospital.

Sarah launched herself out of the chair and walked to the door. "No way I'm gonna move up there by myself!"

And so, four months later, Maudie is tossing the battered briefcase and canvas bag into the back of the van and hauling herself up onto the ripped Naugahyde passenger seat. "What I want you to do, Pete, when we git over there is for you to listen to everthin' that girl an' me says." You nod like a schoolboy. "If she says it's hot, it's hot." She rolls the window up. "Open the dang window. An' if she says it's cold, then jump up and close it. It's cold. Even if it ain't."

You nod again, noting the sparse hair on her legs and the rips in her red Keds sneakers. As you make a right onto Atlantic Drive, Maudie continues, "An' if I say that y'all gotta leave the room, then don't argue with me 'bout this or that, just git outa there. And—"

"I got the point, Maudie," you say with a smile, and as you roll silently down the cottage road, you can see Woody on the top deck waving at the van and then running down to the sand. "Before we get in, Maudie," you whisper, "will you tell me what happens if something goes wrong?"

"Nothin'll go wrong, grampa," she mutters, "just listen to me an' nothin'll go wrong. There ain't nothin' complicated about it. This is the most natural thing in life."

"I'm serious, Maude, what if—"

She makes a noise with her lips. "If somethin' ain't right, Pete, then you'll haul ass up to the pay phone and git me an ambulance!" She shakes her head as if you were the ignorant one; as if all men were somehow ignorant to the obvious ways of the world. "There ain't no guarantees in this life, Mr. Hudson."

Woody is already screaming by the time they pull into the drive. "Where ya been? Where ya been? Sarah's gonna have her baby!"

You knock his forehead with the flat of your hand. "I didn't know that!" Woody looks confused as you take some bills out of your wallet and say, "Now, do me a favor and go get five or six dinners down at the hotel!"

As Maudie waddles up and into the cottage you watch the gangly pony of a new teenager race down the road. "Hey," you call out, "where's Michael?"

"Don't know," Woody shouts over his shoulder, dropping two of the bills and scooting after them on the windswept sand. "He came home and left right away."

"He left a long, long time ago, bub," you say to yourself, and walk into the cottage Brenda had wanted you to stay in so long ago.

The three women are in Sarah's small bedroom. You wait at the door while Jessica and Maude put a pad and new linens on the bed, and then lay out the few instruments and vials from the open briefcase on the top of the painted dresser.

"Git out!" Maude shouts at you, startling you out of a memory of Sarah as a little girl. She is pointing to the door.

"What?"

"Git!" She pushes her finger farther out.

Suddenly flushed, you turn to go get something—anything—a cup of coffee. From the stove you can hear Sarah scream "No!" like a frightened child, and wonder whether you are expected to do something, like burst in on them and kick Maude out and take Sarah to Elizabeth City where she belongs. Something to make it all better.

"She's too young," you whisper with the cup at your lips, when you hear the door open and Jessica walk through the living room and into the kitchen, sink full and dirty pots on the stove. "Everything's fine, Peter. She's about two fingers."

Offended by the words, you can't stop your face from contorting. "You don't know what that means?" You shake your head and shrug sheepishly,

"Where were you—?"

You don't let her finish, holding up your hand like a traffic cop. "Don't give me a hard time, Jessica."

"I'm sorry," she says, pressing her lips together. "Well, she's comin' along. The cervix—you know what a cervix is?" You nod even though you have no idea what a cervix is. "The cervix has to open to ten centimeters and she's at four. A finger is two centimeters."

You nod again, still not following. "I heard the baby's heartbeat, though!" she offers excitedly as if that will make you smile. "You wanna hear?"

You must look like an opossum caught in a flashlight beam.

"Come on," she says, holding out her hand and pulling you behind her like you're the same age as Woody.

Standing at the doorway and seeing Sarah lying there on the small bed with her long cotton shirt from Whalebone Junction up under her swollen breasts, and the sheet barely covering her pubic hair, makes you instantly sorry you had allowed yourself to be dragged back in. You're reaching for the doorknob when you see her bulging belly button.

Now Maude is listening through a stethoscope that seems much too fancy for her. "One fifty," she says proudly. "It's a boy. C'mere." She motions for you to come over to the bed. The lower part of her upper arm jiggles as she says, "Head's down, wanna feel a bottom?"

This is the last thing in the world you want to do, but her rough hand grabbing your wrist and pressing your palm on the top of Sarah's bulging belly leaves you no option. It is warm and hard. "Squeeze it," she orders, "you can't feel nuthin' like that!"

A warm breeze rustles the curtains and blows across your sweating neck. You squeeze, but very gently, glancing away from her belly button and then the dark pubic hairs at the edge of the sheet, finding some relief in Jessica's smirk as she stands by the window.

"Maudie," she calls out, "give him the stethoscope."

You fix your eyes at her smile, relieved that you don't have to say anything, moving one hand from Sarah's belly and wiping your forehead with the back of your wet palm. And once the ear pieces are uncomfortably set, Maude takes the bell and moves it in a circular motion.

At first all you hear are the crackling sounds of the stethoscope being moved to the spot and then being settled around it. Then the scraping sound of fingers pressing down on the bell. Nothing else. You show a fake smile and move to take the plugs from your ears when you hear what sounds like a water pump back on your grandfather's farm outside of Charlotte, and then the rushing of water, the swoosh of a cold brook punctuated by the rapid clap of a piston moving up and down, up and down, when you feel a slap on your knee and the last syllables of an order from Maude: "Move!"

Then Sarah is panting, digging her nails into your forearm, and some hold-your-breath moments later Jessica announces that the contraction lasted forty seconds and was five minutes from the previous one.

And, moments later, without knowing how you got there, you are back in the doorway, hands against both jambs, and Jessica is standing right in front of you. "Move it over, good lookin', I'm comin' through."

Stepping to the side, you feel her brush by and watch over your shoulder as she closes the bathroom door and clicks the lock.

Just then Woody walks in with a pile of Styrofoam cases. "Did she?"

"Nope," you say, walking into the shadowy living room, the fan riffling your soaked shirt. "But I heard the baby's heartbeat," you begin, feeling so awkward being this naked with your son. "It was"—you nod, and nod again—"it was really incredible, Woody . . ." You borrow Jessica's overused word. "Do you want to . . . ?"

Woody grimaces.

"You don't have to. I just thought you might want to check it out . . . go sit down." You point to the table.

You give the boy a chipped china plate and transfer a fried sea trout and a baked potato from the white plastic container.

"Aren't you gonna eat, Dad?"

You place a paper cup of water to the side of the plate. "Not now, Woody. I don't think I could keep anything down." You feel your face wince. "You finish up and I'll drive you over to the Parkers' place . . . unless you want to stay around here."

But before you get to hear Woody's decision, Sarah's moaning drifts in, followed by a high-pitched squeal. And then Maudie's commanding voice: "You can be louder'n that, girl! Screech if ya want; ain't no never mind. This is your day. Scream all ya want, mothergirl."

So you turn away and mumble an easy excuse, walking into the bathroom for no other reason than because you can't face Woody with all that bloody screaming going on. And after flicking on the light and shutting the door, you glance around at the sink and tub and toilet. Everything in need of a scrubbing. In the mirror, you stare intently at your face, noting that you need a shave, patting down your gray-specked hair and thinking that you look weary and old.

In the next moment you suddenly feel lightheaded and unfamiliar, pinching your cheeks the way some people mold clay, pulling them out like a clown and grotesquely wagging your tongue from side to side.

At the unsettling sound of another deep moan from across the hall, you rub the non-existent tears away from your eyes, flip the light on, flush the toilet, wash your hot face and walk back out into the hall.

"Anything?" you say, faking a casual air like you once did in the advertising business, walking in and catching Jessica's eye. She looks angry you think.

"It'll be a while."

You wait, trying and failing to make sense of her anger, intense heat behind your face. "I'm gonna check on Woody," you say, pointing out the door, where you find the boy out on the deck. His plate is untouched. "Not hungry?"

"Nah, I just had lunch a while ago," he lies.

"Well, do you wanna go?"

Woody nods with the upper half of his body. "Let me know when she has it, okay?"

And you put your arm around him, and when the boy leans into the cave of your rounded shoulder, the two of you walk down to the sand and toward the van.

* * *

Five minutes later, just as you wipe your sneakers on the reed mat at the screen door and reach in to flip on the outside lamp, a new sound, a howl, rises from the nearby bedroom, followed by a shriek . . . and Sarah is pleading with Maude and then Jessica to do something. "Do something, Jessica!"

She sounds almost like the thirteen-year-old she used to be, hysterical about the orthodontist.

Unwilling—and maybe unable—to go back into the bedroom just then, you make another cup of Folgers, put in extra sugar, and sit down at the yellow table, both hands around the hot cup, forearms pressed into the sticky aluminum edge, staring at the map of the Outer Banks tacked to the wall behind Michael's seat, wishing you could just run off and follow the barrier islands and the intercoastal waterways all the way to the Keys. Somewhere you won't have to think anymore. Or remember.

When Sarah groans, the reverie is broken. Then she screams out, "Help me!! Daddy!! Please!!" And without thinking you take one last sweet gulp of the cold coffee and push the chair out, striding in toward the storm when Maude orders, "Git outa here!"

But you stand defiantly in the doorway and watch as the old midwife slips a gloved hand under the sheet and Sarah winces before Maude turns again and glowers your way. "I said git!"

Jessica motions with her head. You turn, walking down the short hall toward the bedroom because there's nowhere else to go. And you find some stale Juicy Fruit gum on top of the dresser, looking in the same mirror where you last saw Brenda's face.

Then there is a hand on your shoulder, and you see Jessica where Brenda had been. "Hey, don't take it seriously. Maudie's just like that."

"I know. I know," you say into the mirror. "This is just harder than I thought. So many memories." You shake your head. "So what's happening? How's she doing?"

"Good—real good. Maudie just checked; she's four fingers." You wince again, but she doesn't seem to notice or care. "It'll be pretty soon—let's go on in. I'm sure Sarah wants to see you now."

She disappears from the mirror and when you see her halfway down the hall, you call out, "Have you seen Michael?"

She turns. "No, why?"

"Nothing. He's just not home."

* * *

The bed is empty when you return to Sarah's bedroom. Maude is sitting in the rocker with her eyes closed. Rather than ask, you walk out to find Sarah standing in the living room looking out the front window toward the dunes. She looks no different than a year before, just a bit chunkier in the arms. The white nightshirt with a skull and crossbones across the back comes halfway down her brown thighs. "Maude made me get up. 'Git up,' " she said, imitating the old midwife, "Move her all 'round—git it goin'."

And you laugh, not knowing where the relief comes from. "It's crazy, you know," she says apropos of nothing, "but I can't stop thinking of her." Her voice is as soft and worn as the cotton shirt.

"I know," you whisper, "she would've—" You start to say that she would have been a great comfort, but don't know whether that is true anymore. In the pause, you can hear Jessica chopping ice and scooping it into a glass, the rush of the waves moving up on the other side of the dunes.

"I hardly think of it anymore," she goes on, a tear sliding down her red cheek. "But, you know I still hate her. I hate her." She nods her head. "I really hate her. And Buddy. I thought maybe I'd—"

You don't know what to say, holding your breath, walking over and squeezing her until she suddenly pushes away and plops down on the couch.

It is a long contraction, the soft skin on her smooth face progressively contorted until she loses the steady pattern of chest breathing Maude had insisted upon like a drill sergeant, desperately reaching back for the rhythm and your hand, her nails deep in the spaces between the thin bones, finally letting go of the moan until it's a shriek, her legs shaking violently, her voice hardly recognizable. "Make it stop! Please, Daddy, make it stop! I can't stand it anymore. I hate it I hate it!"

You catch a glimpse of Maude walking your way, then Sarah's eyes wide open in terror, pointing. "Don't you touch me, don't you touch me, you bitch, you, you get me a real doctor. Daddeeeeee, Oh, Oh God, oh God it hurts so much . . ." Her back arches, nails digging into the back of your wrist.

Maude doesn't say anything, just nods your way with a smile spreading across her fat red cheeks.

Half a minute later it is over, a cool breeze fluttering the yellowed curtains. You watch Maude to see what she's going to do, her cow eyes watching Sarah, who is slumped down in an amnesic haze whimpering.

"It's hot!" Sarah demands suddenly, blindly wiping her brow. Maude looks at Jessica and points to the bedroom.

"There's a fan in your room," Jessica says to Sarah, reaching down for her other hand.

"I can't."

"Okay," she says, holding her hands up. "But let's go back there anyway. Just in case. Want some ice?"

Sarah shakes her head, grabbing on to your arm with both hands and pulling her large bulk up with a groan, and you lead her around the scratched coffee table and over to the narrow hall.

But before you make it to her room, she cries,"Oh no! Not another one!" grasping her belly and leaning on the wall. "It's not time, I just did it!"

Jessica looks at her watch. It couldn't have been more than two minutes. From behind, Maude's voice rises like a cowhand herding them along, "Git'er in there!" And then she begins the sharp cadence once again: "Breathe—breathe—breathe—breathe." By the time Sarah makes it to her rumpled bed, she is already losing control, desperately trying to catch up to the pain spreading across her belly with each mounting second until the moaning begins and then the shrieking, the screaming, the pleading, the threats to the fat woman at her feet, the heat over her eyes, the gripping pain in her back; the taste of blood is in your mouth.

Now Jessica fixes Sarah's hair in a ponytail while you wipe her forehead with a wet cloth, the frizzy hairs at the edge smoothed back with the sweeping movement of her hand—before it all starts again. And two minutes later there is the same shock and despair, pleading for more rest, moaning and then shrieking, "I can't stand it!! . . . Please . . . Please!" she begs, "Daddeeeee!!!"

But all she gets is "Breathe, breathe, breathe . . ." from the red hole in the round face between her legs.

"I'm gonna shit!" she cries out in panic.

"G'head and shit, child, no never mind."

"Noooo!" she cries. "It's burning! It's burning—it hurts so much—Jesseeee—I'm gonna shit!"

Then the voice again, sure and deep and stable: "This is it, honey-bun, just bear down when ya feel the urge." Maude pulls the sheet away and you glance away, over at Jessica, who is standing by the window, and you hear a grunt that is so deep and so hard and so full of life and death that you get dizzy. "MaMaaaaaaaaa!" the girl cries.

This is when Maude orders Sarah to grab the outside of her thighs and "Bear down, girl." "And Peter," she yells across the bed, "c'mere and git her shoulders an' lift her up."

You do it, relieved to be behind your daughter, holding her up until she falls back into your arms, the contraction spent. "That's it mother, take a res'," Maudie says, sticking her fat fingers in an open jar of Vaseline.

A moment later, Sarah is panting again, and Maude is yelling at you to lift her up while she coos at the girl, all the while making a smooth ring around the lips of her swollen vagina, moving round and round even as Sarah screams out, "I can't wait—I'm gonna push!"

"That's it—then push 'er outa there!" The bulging beneath her pubic bone grows rounder and rounder like a tornado, a black lumpy circle of blood and hair and bone emerging with another soul-shaking grunt from the black hole deep in Sarah's throat.

"Push it out honey. That's it—Peter," she snarls, "don't just stand there like a statue, git 'er up!"

You push her up but it's already too late; Sarah is leaning back in your arms, her chest heaving up and down.

"One more time, Sarah girl," comes a softer voice than you've ever heard from Maude, "wait till ya jes' cain't hole on no longer and then bear on down, sweetheart."

"Here it comes, here it comes . . ."

"Pick 'er up, Dad! Grab yer legs, girl!"

"Oh," she wails, "it stings! It stings! Oh Christ, it stings!"

"Push, baby! Push 'er out—keep 'er up, Father. Take a deep breath and push!" Sarah grabs her thighs and heaves down, her face straining as if she is being dragged through the dark ocean, Maude's strong hand covering her opening. "Push!"

You hear Jessica yelling "Push!" from the window.

"Tha's it, one more big 'un!"

And Sarah heaves into the contraction with a massive grunt that shakes your soul. "Now, pant, pant, pant, just like I told ya t'do! Pant, pant, pant." Maude's hand, cupped around the bulging darkness, soon fills with the back of a black skull the size of a fist, purple and bloody and slippery, a tiny squashed face—eyes closed, chin up against Sarah's wet pubic bone.

You turn to see Jessica holding on to the ledge of the window behind her with both hands.

Sarah stretches up to see, but Maude tells her to lie back, that there will just be one more contraction, and that she has to listen to her. "Wha's gonna happen next is—"

But before she can go on, Sarah is reaching for her legs and heaving down again, another growl deep in her throat. The tiny head in Maude's hands begins to rotate toward the inside of Sarah's bloody white thigh. "Good, good, good . . . now when I tell ya, pant, don't push!"

"I can't stop mys—" A grunt escapes before she can push the words from her mouth.

"That's good, now PANT, PANT! PANT!" Maude says, now

panting along with her.

"I can't." She blows and blows and blows down against her chest and then bears down again.

"Pant, pant, pant . . . ," the old woman orders, just barely tilting the baby's head down, exposing a frail wrinkled shoulder, and then quickly tilting his head up while Sarah lets out one final massive groan and a tiny boy baby with an enormous scrotum slides into Maude's waiting hands, bluish and bloody, covered with a cheesy substance all over his lifeless body. The cord continues to pulsate.

"He's not breathing!" Sarah cries out.

"He'll breathe," Maude scolds, holding his head down in one arm and sweeping her finger through his tiny mouth. She reaches for a gauze pad on the other side of the bed and wipes it roughly across the tiny face, watching carefully as the infant gasps convulsively and starts to cough, the cough turning into a tiny squeak of a cry, the baby boy slowly turning pink in the midwife's hands and wailing at the shock of life.

A few seconds pass, each of which might have lasted all the ages of the earth, and no one says a word, everyone listening to these first sounds of life, until Sarah reaches down for her son. "Brendan," she whispers.

Maude suctions the baby's mouth quickly with a bulb syringe and passes him over her mushy belly like a bouquet of flowers. "He's a beauty. Giv 'im yer breast, honey."

Sarah looks up from her son to you. She looks like a schoolgirl again and you smile, heart thudding, and kiss her gently on her wet forehead.

Now Sarah hikes her sweaty sweatshirt over her large round breasts."Just tetch his mouth to yer nipple." And at the touch of the erect pink nipple on his wet cheek, Brendan Hudson opens his tiny mouth and sucks it in with a slight tug of his bumpy bald head, still attached to the pulsing cord traveling down and up through the darkness between his mother's legs.

Jessica comes over crying and hugs Sarah, kissing the nursing infant. And then moves to the head of the bed and kisses you, the taste of birth on her lips.

* * *

Early the following morning out on the beach as the sun emerges over the unusually quiet ocean, Jessica tells you very gently, very slowly, that you are going to have to marry her if you want her to stay.

Part III

Chapter 12

Spring 1975

You thought that the opening of *The Island Weekly* office in the empty storage room next to Austin's Bait and Tackle in Waves was as good an excuse as any for a big celebration. The party was to be held two weeks before Easter, when everyone on the island was on the verge of recovering from the fluish effects of cottage fever, before the first wave of fishermen and tourists would drive most of the locals back inside their cottages and summer businesses.

You had ordered twenty cases of cheap champagne, six kegs of Budweiser and bushels and bushels of jimmies and shrimp; arranged for a girl band from Nags Head named Penny Farthing and the Cheapskates to play for three hours; and invited everyone on the island to the party on the first page of the March 12 edition of the *Weekly.*

A couple hundred locals from Hatteras Village to Rodanthe show up, including the feuding Burris boys who haven't seen each other since sometime after the Korean War. Some folks even come in from Chapel Hill after reading about the party in the newspaper.

Sarah is right in the center of things, proudly showing off your nearly-ten-month-old grandson, who probably looks a little too much like Buddy Neuse for your comfort, right down to his small ears. Buddy is in Germany the last anyone heard. And Sarah does not let him—or any Neuses—know that he has a son.

Woody has walked down to the celebration with Mrs. Parker and

Covington. Even Michael shows up. Nobody in the family has actually seen him in three days, though there was evidence in the kitchen that he had blown through several times. He arrives with the other members of the Cape Hatteras School starting five. They had made it to the semi-finals of the state championship just two weeks before, and each one wears a dark blue windbreaker with a large basketball on the back and their record (25-1) right in the middle. They have come looking for beer—and girls.

Early in the afternoon, you gather the kids near the breezy front deck and have Hal Kaminski, the staff photographer, take five shots of the smiling happy family in front of the sign in the window. You kow it is a lot of BS, especially with all the family had been through, but you are as close to happy as you've been in years and you still hope that Michael will forgive you for your failures.

The following week, you place a sharp five-by-seven copy of the best print on the front page of *The Island Weekly* under the sixty-point headline:

HUDSONS OPEN OFFICE IN WAVES

You are standing in the middle of the photograph holding Brendan, a broad smile across your face, your arms around Sarah and Woody. Michael stands next to Woody, staring, expressionless, straight into the lens.

* * *

Jessica does not show up. In fact, Jessica Walsh may have been the only resident of the three towns of Rodanthe, Waves, and Salvo who is not there.

You had called her earlier in the day asking her to please reconsider and join the family at the celebration. "Please, Jessica. It's as much for you as for anyone around here; we couldn't have done any of this without you."

She apologizes and tells you that she doesn't feel well and is going to spend the day in bed. Of course you know she is lying, but you are content for the time being to accept what she says. At least, you think, she didn't tell you no.

* * *

The last time you had seen Jessica Walsh, two weeks before the party, the two of you were out at the end of the pier just staring down into the rolling swells. She told you then with a quivering voice, long hair blowing against her red cheeks, that it was no longer simply about getting married. Brendan's birth had woken her up. She wanted to have a baby—and her time was running out. "I can't wait for you any longer, Peter . . . I love you, I love you more than you might ever know, but I can't wait around for you to . . ."

It didn't seem to matter that the two of you had warmed countless cold, windy nights that winter with plans to get married as soon as you got it together to move the *Weekly* out of the cottage. But neither of you had ever mentioned a baby. At least you never had.

You swallowed hard at Jessica's unexpected declaration, leaning on the rail and staring out at the same old arc of water and sky. You saw the fat red head of a loggerhead turtle maybe a quarter of a mile away, but didn't have the strength or the will to point it out, to shift the current.

"Hey," you said, laying a mottled hand over hers on the rail, "let's just take this one step at a time. I thought we had a big breakthrough last summer . . . and one breakthrough a year is enough for anyone, right?" You flashed your best Rosslyn smile. "Jessica, sweetheart, you know I'm really looking forward to us getting married . . . but I've been through too much to start all over again with a baby. I'm too old, Jessica. I'm a grandfather . . . ," you said, brightening your smile, looking for her eyes. "I feel like I was shipwrecked on this island—and I just want to be with you."

She covered her top lip with the lower one and faced into the wind. You took her cool hand in both of yours. "Let's just get married and be together forever, the two of us. I don't think I can start all over again."

She didn't say anything, just slipped her hand from yours and turned away, walking alone down the entire thousand-foot shaking pier like a wave headed to the eroding shore.

* * *

"Just like Brenda," you tell Billy Austin, a few nights later in the pier house. Billy is Jay Austin, owner of Austin's Bait and Tackle in Salvo, and is the one person on the island whom you can talk to besides Jessica, and that's only because Billy is generally too drunk to disagree with what you have to say.

You think it was Jessica who had told you that Billy had gone to Yale right after two soul-shattering tours in Okinawa, the first Islander that anyone could remember to go to an Ivy, where he became a poet and a drunk. When he finally returned to Buxton, he gave up everything else in his life except beer and writing poetry he never showed anyone. His younger brother Mac, who owned the business, took care of him.

Trapped inside his daily stupor, Billy urges you to write about it. "Get it out in the air, Peter m'boy." So you go back to the cottage and in a poetic rush of emotion write what seems at first like an innocently lyrical piece about the beach being eroded by the sensuous lick of the sea, slowly swallowing the sand, inch by inch, until there is nothing but water rolling endlessly over silent land. It is the first creative writing you had done since Chapel Hill, and to your everlasting shame, you place it on the editorial page of the *Weekly*, hoping Jessica will see it and finally understand.

* * *

After the Grand Opening Celebration is over, you spend days driving up and down Highway 12 between the protected areas of the National Seashore, unable to get Jessica from your mind, aching again to feel her smooth legs draped over yours on the couch as the two of you read the night away in delicious silence. But rumbling past her battered cottage for the fourth time and then turning once again at the start of the protected Park Service area, you finally understand there is no hope.

So you step on the gas, push the pedal to the floor, and by the time the van whistles past Jessica's place the speedometer is quavering violently between seventy-five and ninety-five, the steering wheel trembling in your clenched fists. At Raymond Sawyer's sign you jam on the brakes like a drunk teenager, fishtailing into the empty parking lot at the White Heron Campground. You need something. A Hershey's. Potato chips. Something.

Inside, Mary Ellen, the chunky, unmarried, thirtyish daughter of the owners, Bull and Roxanne, chews on a celery stick and tells you with too much exuberance about what a great party you had thrown. No doubt having noticed—as did practically everyone else at the party—that Jessica was not there, you figure that's why Mary Ellen invites you for a family dinner the next day. You thank her graciously and, with a laugh, invent "a million and one obligations over the next few weeks to pay for that damn party, Mary Ellen!" tapping her pinkish white arm just above her bent elbow.

She giggles, as you knew she would.

Then you walk through the three aisles, buying simply to look purposeful. So by the time you return to the smiling and primping

Mary Ellen behind the counter, you have an armful of unnecessary supplies: ice cream, orange juice, cereal, candy bars, a crumb cake, light bulbs. And then you drive slowly back through Rodanthe and Waves and into Salvo, stopping in the sand in front of Jessica's cottage.

Jessica opens the door wearing a faded cotton T-shirt and a pair of ripped jeans. She doesn't move, just looks at you through the screen. "I thought you might want some dessert," you say, holding a grocery bag out for her inspection.

She remains staring at you until you lower the bag. "No thanks, Peter," she says, "I'm just not feeling up to it."

Resisting an urge to move a strand of hair from across her cheek, you say, "I'm really sorry, Jess. I really am. How about just some company?"

Jessica shakes her head. "No, Peter, I'm sorry. I can't do this anymore. I just can't. I've got to get on with my life."

She starts to close the flat, windowless door when you speak into the diminishing slice of her life: "I just don't know what I'm doing without you. I'm just driving up and down the goddamn road."

"Go away, Peter. Please."

You stand there staring through the stretched screen, sure that if she can just see your pain she will at least open the door further and maybe even invite you in.

"If I let you in," she starts, and you suddenly feel a lightness behind your unwavering eyes, ". . . if I let you in, we'll just go on until I can't stand it anymore and start this all over again—or worse, we'll just go on. It's too hard, Peter. Please just go away."

She turns and walks off toward the kitchen then, leaving the door half open behind her.

"Please wait!" you call and watch her shake her head and wave you off with one hand.

Alone on the dark porch, you reach into the bag and throw the ice cream and cake and candy bars over the edge of the peeling railing, and hear the muffled sounds as each one hits the cool sand.

* * *

That night you drink yourself to sleep in a hard swivel chair in the new office, feet up on the used metal secretary's desk, tingling hands behind your head, wondering how your life has once again come to be such a pitiable mess.

You hold a jelly glass half full of bourbon up in the air and, more than half drunk, repeated verbatim the toast you had received from Ed McCann at the Rotary Club luncheon in Rosslyn for your work for the United Way: "To a very good man whose life is a model to follow for us all!"—and wash it down with another inch of Jim Beam.

And the following day, except for a brief trip over to the cottage to mess up the bed and get a very groggy Woody off to school—pausing briefly at Sarah's door when you think you hear Brendan stirring—you stay at the new office, clearing, cleaning, sorting files, putting up bulletin boards, making photocopies of articles on the new rental machine, creating a primitive darkroom in the bathroom, writing copy, editing, updating subscription lists . . . until Sarah makes a worried call in the middle of the evening wondering what has happened to you.

You apologize and tell her you'll be home in fifteen minutes, and then walk into the darkened cottage hours later at 11:45. Sarah is already asleep.

The next morning you are up before six to run the beach and then, as usual, leave for the empty office as soon as Woody wakes for school. The new office, which resembles a dusty junk room more than a business, quickly becomes your refuge—from Jessica mostly, but also Michael, the memory of Brenda that resides in Sarah's eyes, the shame of your longing to get away from Woody, and everyone who wants anything of you except to place an ad.

And so for the next month or so, you will be in the office by 7:15 and will still be there when Danny Austin, Jr. closes the store for his father at 10 p.m. There is nowhere else for you to go. Seven days a week.

One night Sarah calls and reminds you that this was the way it used to be in Rosslyn when her mom complained that you worked all the time.

"I'm not the same person I was back then" is all you could offer in return.

She says she can't for the life of her remember how it "used to be" since you were all stranded down there. "I don't even recognize myself in the mirror these days . . . and I probably couldn't even fill out a missing person's report on you."

"I'll make it up to you," you said. "I promise, Sarah."

"Never mind," she answers, adding, "everyone's doing okay without you."

She is right. Woody seems fine over at Covington's house, where he spends every afternoon and all weekend, and, as Sarah once muttered, Michael seemsd happy enough to be "providing stud service to every girl on the Outer Banks." More important, though, he has been offered a no-guarantees partial scholarship to Chapel Hill and since then hadn't spent any time at the cottage other than to sleep and drop off his sports copy. And pick up a check.

And Sarah, despite feeling isolated and a little closed in, is enjoying motherhood more than she—or you—had ever imagined. Mrs. Sharp up on Coquina Drive takes Brendan for a couple hours each day and that pretty much keeps Sarah from climbing the walls. That's when she'd goes over to the office to take care of her columns—and walk the beach.

Chapter 13

In early June, you run into Jessica at the high school graduation ceremonies in Buxton. Michael's graduation. It's the first time you're seeing her since she walked away and left you standing on her porch.

You should be sitting in one of the folding chairs set up on the sandy lawn. But since you are covering the ceremony for the *Weekly*, you're walking by the makeshift stage when you spot her.

Both of you flush. There are no words, Jessica's eyes opening wide. Time stops—the hammer of the howling wind silenced, the waves flat—and all that is needed is a word, just a word, to get it all moving again.

"Sooo, Peter . . . ," she begins, leaping into the void, and suddenly people are moving all around. "How you doing?"

"One foot in front of another," you say, arms at your side, aching to reach out and hold her close. "You?"

She shrugs. "Looking forward to lying on the beach."

You don't know what to say next, so you just nod and smile. Then there is nothing again, the two of you stranded in the eye of your own personal hurricane, when Jessica breaks the veil again. "So, what do you hear from M. Shire?"

At first you're confused. Then it makes sense and you allow a thin smile to part your tight lips. "She—uh, he?—just got a renewal notice from me . . . ," you say, shaking your head, instantly sorry that you hadn't come up with something witty and engaging. It isn't even true.

"Oh, well that's good . . . I guess. Is he or she still living in . . . Milwaukee, was it?"

For no good reason you can remember, C. Pedro, M. Shire, and K. Trapani had become a great source of easy good-natured fun for the two of you during the winter when all was well and Jessica was still working on the newspaper. You two had imagined C.P. as a Connecticut Yankee who escaped New England society to fish and drink on the Outer Banks; K.T. as a widow, a music professor at Smith with three daughters, who had spent her North Carolina childhood summers on Hatteras; and M.S., as an exotic dancer from New Orleans who cleaned up her act, married an accountant from Asheville, NC, sent in a change of address to Chicago, IL, then another to Milwaukee, WI.

But for no other reason than that Jessica found the change of addresses so odd, you two focused on Margo Shire to fill the long hours of a desolate winter with speculations about her lot in life. It was unusual enough to have received a subscription request from Louisiana—and then Milwaukee—but as the requests came from a single woman (there was no other name on the check, a left-handed slant to a scribbled signature), it became all the more mysterious.

Although you had asked around and at the two real-estate offices, no one in the three towns knew anything about M. Shire. Even Mary Ellen over at the KOA, who seemed to know as much as anybody about the comings and goings on the island, couldn't help you.

During that long and particularly bitter winter on the island, everybody trapped inside their wind-creaky homes watching grainy television screens and reading endless mystery novels, Margo Shire became your favorite game to while away the hours. You happily imagined her as a hooker, an elegant aristocrat, a dyke, a writer, a transvestite, a killer stalking the whereabouts of some innocent victim on the island, a wilted flower who yearned unrequitedly for the day when her true love, Bruce Hill, would return to the scene of their great passion when he was stationed at Keesler Field in Biloxi. The stories were endless, or at least they went on until two weeks before the party when Jessica walked away from you on the shifting pier.

And now at the graduation ceremonies, M. Shire again provides a connection. Something.

Anxious to keep the conversation going as harried teachers and administrators brush along behind you, nearly paralyzed in Jessica's presence, you blurt out an unrehearsed invitation to join the family for a dinner celebration down at the Tiki in Salvo "for old times' sake" and add that "Sarah would love to see you."

Now it's Jessica's turn to be speechless, her mouth open, back of her hand against her forehead, asking if it's suddenly so hot and saying that she needs to sit down.

You lead her so naturally by the elbow to a seat in the shade, which soon enough becomes the two of you sitting side by side, and then your arm sliding around her shoulder, her head resting on your shoulder . . . and twelve hours later, waking up in each other's arms, the baby wailing for the breast in the small room down the hall.

* * *

After your eyes open, sunlight streaming through the fluttering curtains, Jessica sits up and says that she has decided that as long as she has broken every Norman Vincent Peale–inspired affirmation to keep desire within herself, the best thing to do is to give you until the end of the summer to make up your mind, and if you still can't do it, then she will just leave the island. "There just won't be any other way to save myself but to go away." She adds as an afterthought, "I can always find a teaching position in Raleigh or even out near Asheville. And in the meantime, it's summer vacation and

I won't even mention it until the summer is over. I'll just help out in the office in the mornings and spend my afternoons on the beach."

You are frankly humiliated to be spoken to like a child, but too happy, too filled with gratitude for her news. All you can do is take her hand and press it to your cheek. And then go off for your daily run over the dunes.

Chapter 14

August 1975

A flushed pregnant woman, barely more than a girl, knocks and before there's an answer, steps into the air-conditioned *Island Weekly* office in Waves. "Jesus, what a relief!" she says, wiping the sweat from her thin face, red frizzy hair pulled up into a ridiculous-looking spout at the top of her head.

You look up from the pasteup table and see an egg-shaped lady in a ruffled pink maternity blouse and flowered polyester stretch shorts waddling her way through the maze of papers and cartons full of folders.

"What can I do for you?" You smile conditionally.

"Are you a Mr. Hudson? Mind?" she asks, pointing to an orange vinyl office chair and plopping herself down before you can respond. Legs spread wide open, splash of white panties at the top of her pressed thighs. "Damn, it's hot!" she says, not seeming to mind your stare.

"Yes?"

"Well," she locates a piece of gum in the back of her mouth and begins chewing again, "my name is Sharon Ford, me and my old man are stayin' over at the KOA and he's been out fishin' every goddamn day this week and I been jus' about bonkers with nothin' t'do 'cept sittin' on the friggin' hot beach or over in the back of the camper—Jesus, what do you all do here? Even the friggin' TV's on the fritz—but anyway . . ." She sighs then and wipes her forehead with the back of her freckled hand. "You don't wanna know nothin' about that, though—I jus' got so bored that I thought I'd try to look up a ol' fren a'mine. Well, not a fren, just a . . . I dunno what the hell she was."

You glance over at the foot-high pile of folders on your desk and then back to the young woman lifting her massive breasts up off her equally massive belly. You can't take your eyes off of all the girth on that skinny frame. "So?" you say, finally looking away and leaning back in the chair.

She scowls and cups both breasts. "So, when I was dancin' on Bourbon Street these shook up more dicks than you could count. I could see 'em pop right out there on the sidewalk when Charlie opened the door to let 'em get a peek." She wipes her forehead again before continuing. "Anyway, things change, and the lady over at the campground store says you might be able to help me find her—I wanna tell her I'm havin' a kid."

Staring hard into her red face, you find nothing that you recognize; she looks to be the same age as Sarah, but is someone who has clearly lived a lot longer. You lift your eyebrows to let her know you're waiting.

"Yeah, well, the lady said you probably knew more about people comin' and goin' than anyone around here . . . there's always some busybody watchin' out every place you go. Me? I don't care, easy come easy go."

"So . . . who are you looking for?" Unable to hide your impatience, you are about to make up an excuse about an interview you have to do.

She snaps the gum on the back of her teeth. "Just an old friend, Margo. Margo Shire—we useta live in the same boardin' house down in New Orleans. My old man moved us to Macon last year to get away from my old job."

You are stunned into an uncontrollable smile, leaning forward and letting the two front legs of your chair clap the linoleum. "Margo Shire?" You reach for the phone. "You really know Margo Shire?"

"Sure, we was friends"—she is smiling now as if she had just won an award—"and I remember that she usedta live here or somethin'. Is she round here now? Y'know where I can find her?"

You can't stop yourself from grinning, already enjoying the thought of telling all this to Jessica, your finger in the rotary dial. "Do you know where she is?"

She glares at you then. "No! What the hell d'you think I'm doing here!"

You erase the smirk on your face and begin: "Well, the truth is that I'm very intrigued by Ms. Shire, but I really don't know her at all, except—"

She cuts you off. "'Cept what?"

"Except, she subscribes to this paper from an address in Milwaukee, Wisconsin. I know the address by heart—it's on North Newhall Street."

"Well, for shit's sakes"—she drops her breasts—"she didn't go home. Why the fuck did she go all the way up there to my poor excuse for a hometown? Maybe she looked up my Ma. I don't friggin' believe it!"

"I'm sorry, where'd you know her from?" you say, refreshed and beaming with expectation. "Say," you add, getting yourself up from the desk, "can I get you something to drink, ma'am?"

"Yeah, get me a Dr. Pepper." She seems pleased to be treated like a lady.

You point a finger and say, "Don't move," jogging out the door and over to Austin's. You bring back two sodas and a bag of pretzels; then listen in chilling silence to Sharon's story, full of full-tilt memory lapses and very odd embellishments, of what she remembers about Margo Shire's trip from the Outer Banks all the way to a rooming house in New Orleans, Louisiana.

* * *

Sharon's globe of a face is flushed and orange as her frizzy hair, growing angrier and more orange before she finally pushes herself up out of the vinyl chair in *The Island Weekly* office. You have not uttered a sound for at least a minute since she finished her story; you're just sitting behind the desk with your chin in the sling of thumb and forefinger, the wires in your brain sizzling and erupting in small flash fires here and there until finally, shaking your skull, jiggling loose the burnt ends of more than a thousand days, you say, "I'm sorry, but I really don't know what to say, Mrs. . . . ?"

She won't help you, her thin lips pressed together. So you go on, "But all I can tell you is that Margo Shire doesn't live around here. I don't even know who she is."

"Well," she mutters, plopping the empty soda can on the desk and watching as it tips over and rolls to the dusty vinyl floor. "You can't blame no one for tryin'. I don't know what the fuck I wanted with her, anyway. She was a snooty little bitch. Thanks for nothin'."

When she yanks open the door and the hot humid air is sucked into the office, she snarls, "Jesus H. Christ! I'm back in the Quarter!" But you can't find any more words, even just to tell her to shut the damn door, watching an apparition fill up the wavering space between the jambs, hearing only the rales of your own labored breathing and the whine of a steady stream of morning tires along Highway 12.

You keep your eyes on her, though, watching her swing herself flatfooted out onto the deck and slam the flimsy door behind her like an angry afterthought. The drone of the clunky GE air conditioner and the steady drip in the pan on the floor replace the whine of the tires.

Alone with your confusion and fury—and something akin to terror—you yank open the bottom desk drawer, pull out a fifth of Jim Beam and pour a couple of fingers into a jelly glass, the bourbon sharp in your mouth, burning your esophagus all the way down. After another finger and then another, you lean back in the swivel chair in a near stupor, finally beginning to catch up with the flash fires erupting inside your head.

You envision your brain as the tangled bunches of hot sparking wires stuffed beneath the dashboard of a car stalled on the side of the road. And before you know it, the phone is in your hand and you're holding the heavy black receiver up in the air as if it might tell you something.

For a moment you think you can hear her voice through the incessant beep signaling a phone off the hook. It is only then, your finger aiming for the button to stop the siren, you realize that you not only don't know the New Orleans area code, but can't remember your wife's name. Either name.

In fact, it is only when you find the area code in the thin Dare County telephone book that you remind yourself that she had moved to Milwaukee.

Moments later, a dozen thin telephone book pages crumpled up across the floor, you dial Information, shove an unlit cigarette in your dry mouth, and wait for the connection. "Margo Shire, North Newhall Street," you mumble, and with a shaking, sweaty hand scribble the numbers on last week's paper.

Chapter 15

The first time you call, the phone rings twice and, just as life too often imitates bad movies, you hang up in a panic. Five minutes later when your pulse has slowed at least to the point where you are no longer afraid that your pounding heart will explode, you finally light the soggy cigarette and draw in two quick drags, your lungs recoiling.

The second time the line is busy; the repeating busy signal buzzes against your skull twenty or thirty times.

On the third try you gulp a mouthful of bourbon as soon as the ringing begins, forcing it back over your tonsils so you can speak over the thumping in your throat when someone answers.

"Hello?" a female voice asks.

Your heart is now thudding in your throat. You can't speak. Then a click.

You hold the receiver out away from your head and then drop it in the cradle as if it were contaminated, your hand poised midair, gesturing through the hot air as if there is an audience.

You can't get yourself out of the office quickly enough—the one place where you get respite from the rest of the world is suddenly poisoned—and you slam the door behind you without thinking to turn off the air conditioner or the lights or the coffee machine, drive crazy-reckless over to the empty cottage, and skid into the narrow driveway, one wheel sinking in the sand.

All you want to do is get up the steps, but finding yourself hanging on to the rail out of breath, out of air, you barely manage to pull yourself up by the splintery two-by-six, step by heavy step, all the way up to the deck where you open your mouth to scream . . . and nothing comes out before you yank the torn screen door, step into the cool darkness, and find your voice. "Jesssssica!!!"

But the cottage is empty. As you are to soon find out, Jessica, Sarah, and Brendan are sprawled on the empty beach talking about Sarah's plans to go off to Chapel Hill in the fall and get her life going somewhere, anywhere, other than Rodanthe—so she can stop being the Hudson family's twenty-year-old mother and wife.

Leaning your way toward the new phone on the wall in the kitchen, you pick up the receiver and, seconds later, hang it up.

The refrigerator is just a reach away. As soon as you pull open the door, a blast of cool air moves across your chest and you slam it shut, bottles rattling, a pencil rolling off the dusty top.

Then, turning, you take a pot from the stove and put it in the sink, grab a pack of Luckys from the open cupboard, rip off the entire top, pull out three and drop two that stick to your wet fingers, strike wet match after wet match, and throw the duds down to the floor.

When the ravaged cigarette is finally lit, you spit the tobacco off your tongue and push back through the screen, lumbering out toward the dunes, each step in the loose sand heavier than the one that came before. Your wet shirt clings to your sweaty skin as you start to run, but you are stopped each time after one or two steps, chest heaving, sweat scratching your eyes.

At the top of the dunes, you see a blurred semblance of what might have been Woody, Covington, Sarah, and Brendan in Jessica's arms.

The one who looks like Woody is pointing out beyond the pier. And right before you are sure you will faint, you sit down heavily in the tall sea oats.

A minute or two later, you open your eyes. You don't know if you fainted. But in a moment of stark awareness, you see the one who had to have been Jessica pass the baby over to the one who'd be Sarah and then bend over to shake a towel downwind as if she were getting ready to go back to the cottage. And it is just then, sensing some unformed but imminent danger, you roll to the side like a little boy playing war, get yourself up in a crouch and race all the way back to the road.

To the hot van.

Out to Highway 12.

* * *

Locked inside the contaminated newspaper office in Waves for the entire night, you try to clear your head with what is left of the first fifth of Jim Beam; and proceed to cloud it all over again with another bottle you keep hidden in the back of the metal file cabinet.

Then every twenty minutes on the dot for three hours you call the Milwaukee number, hanging up silently each time Brenda answers the phone . . . sitting there in the dark, dusty office with your aching finger pressed on the button until you have enough oxygen to try it all over again.

After an hour of busy signals, you call the cottage just to hear the ringing and then the sandy quality of Jessica's voice. Sarah answers, though, and she sounds so much like her mother that you almost pound the receiver into the cradle. But you take a deep breath and, sounding as off-handed as you can muster, you tell Sarah that there is an enormous amount of work to be done, and you won't be back home until very late.

She hangs up on you without saying good-bye or offering to get Jessica, angry—as she has so often been lately—at your obsessive devotion to the newspaper.

Doesn't matter now. Moments later, you're yanking again at 4-1-4 on the rotary dial. The infuriating busy signals continue for perhaps another hour, and by then all that matters in your life is getting through just one more time. You no longer care if she answers, just as long as the phone rings—just to let you know she hasn't taken the phone off the hook and run off again.

At one point you pick up a conch shell that Woody had painted for you to hold down papers in the endless breeze, and heave it across the room. It blows a ragged hole through the Sheetrock, dropping down between the studs and out of sight.

* * *

"Hello?"

You push out the words as one wrenches out a rusted nail from a fence post. "Brenda . . ."

She knows instantly. Of course. "Oh my . . . I should have . . . Peter? . . . Peter?"

You can see her tilt her head, brush her hair back. There is a man's voice in the background. You hear her light a cigarette.

"Say something, dammit!"

"Oh Peter, I don't know . . . what to say." Tears flood her voice; she is blowing out a puff of smoke.

"Say something," you mutter and let the air go quiet.

"Don't hang up!" she blurts out finally. "Please! I don't know! I just can't think."

"How could you?"

"I . . ." There is another drag. "How did you . . ." she begins, but stops.

"How could you?"

"I didn't mean to!" she cries. "I really didn't mean to." Her voice is moist and thick. "It just happened; how did you find me?"

You shake your head as if she is right there in Waves. "Does it matter?"

Her voice now just above a whisper. "I guess not. Are you okay? Are the children?"

You take a last swig of the bourbon and throw the glass across the room, shattering it against the cedar wall.

"I don't . . . I don't know what to say—I'm so sorry, Peter, I'm so sorry . . ." She is sobbing now.

You don't answer. Can't locate the words.

After a while her sobs begin to subside and the phone is being jostled as another cigarette is lit. "Are you still there?"

You don't answer, but your panting breath lets her know you are still listening.

You can hear her shallow breaths.

"I, I can't talk, Peter." Her voice breaks through the scratchy silence. "I can't think. I can't think. Let me write you a letter to explain. I've started so many. Please just let me do it that way, and then we can talk again. I'll do it right away, tonight. I promise." There is another long drag on the cigarette.

"No." Though you don't know what you mean by that.

"I know I don't deserve anything, Peter, but please please please don't tell the children if they don't already know. Please let me do it."

Then you find your voice. "Don't you fucking dare, Brenda. You've done enough to them. I'll—"

"I'm sorry," she whines all over again, "I'm sorry, I'm so sorry, I'll write to you, and then we can talk. Is that okay?"

Fifteen seconds later she shatters the silence. "Please tell me, Peter, is that okay?" She sniffs. "Please say s—"

But your finger presses on the button, holding it down, the circle imprinting your soft skin while the wires in your skull begin to pop and sizzle. A building exploding in flames.

* * *

By daybreak, the burning lamp on the desk losing its glow, you float through successive waves of blinding hatred, remorse, self-condemnation, even a strange kind of concern for Brenda's well-being, followed by cool indifference ("She's dead," you mutter, pouring the last drop of the last bottle of bourbon into a paper cup).

At some point you land cheek down on the cluttered desk, snot dripping from your nose, imagining driving up to Norfolk to catch a plane, then a cab to some seedy apartment in Milwaukee, and barging in on her, a man in her bed. You see yourself bounding across some kind of Victorian-appointed room and grabbing the man by the hair—a ponytail; had Sharon told you?—and picking him up and pushing him screaming like some pansy ass through the decrepit screen window, ending with a loud bloody thump on the sidewalk below.

The words never come in the dream, just the sharp slap of your hand across her pleading face, your fingers on her bare shoulders throwing her to the dirty floor, the hollow thud of your shoe bouncing off her ribs.

* * *

Jessica startles you when she pushes open the door to the cold messy office late the next morning, and you lurch for the arms of the chair to keep from flipping over backwards. You squint over at her. The office is too bright, and the Sunday-morning traffic whooshes by until she swings the waterlogged door shut behind her and sits at the edge of a desk across the long room.

You must look green and sickly because she doesn't give you an earful of the speech she'd apparently been rehearsing all night.

"Did you spend the whole night here?" she asks incredulously, just then noticing the gaping hole in the wall. "Peter, what the hell happened there?"

"Oh shit, I forgot about that," you say, rubbing the tingling sleep from your legs.

"Do you wanna talk about it?"

You shake your head—you don't know why—and then hold out your hand, a frayed lifeline from a drowning man. "Come here, I'm really glad to see you. You're a sight for sore eyes." You rub them as soon as you say it, now feeling the day-old growth around your mouth.

She looks startled, a smile breaking through like the sun outside the office. "Well, they certainly look sore. You look like a bum, ya know. You sure you don't wanna talk about it?" She is walking your way.

You shake your head again and reach out across the desk for a hand. "Jessica."

"Yeah?" she says, her voice suddenly like a child's.

You blow out a long thin breath as if you have just inhaled a cigarette and look up at her. She looks fresh and beautiful. "Do you still love me?"

"What do you mean?"

"Just that. Do you love me?"

Jessica nods, a quivering smile emerging across her lips. "I don't know why, but"—the smile broadens—"yes, I do." The smile disappears. "You know that I do."

"My whole life is a meaningless mess without you, Jessica. If I haven't made such a horse's ass out of myself that you'd never consider being my wife, will you still marry me, in spite of who I am?"

* * *

"I will," she whispers a few weeks later, looking first at the cranky old Justice of the Peace, Jimmie Henderson from Manteo, and then over at you. The sun is just coming up. The ocean rolls gently beneath everyone standing at the far end of the pier, close enough to hear the breakers fall languidly onto the sand.

You smile at your gorgeous bride. You can feel the muscles in your jaw flickering, watching the fluttering of her gauzy white dress and her hair waving in the wind.

"Do you, Peter Hudson, take Jessica Walsh to be your lawfully wedded wife, to love and to cherish, in sickness and in health, in good times and bad, till death do you part?"

"I will." Your voice is deep and dry. Jessica's eyes are wet, strands of hair across her mouth.

After the sacred pronouncement, the two of you turn to face the four smiling people who joined you on the pier that early morning. You had gasped when you saw Sarah and Brendan. She was wearing Brenda's white dress that you had brought back from Rosslyn, thinking at the time that it was hers.

You then step away from the recurring nightmare to hug Woody, whose eyes are still red from the night before, the first night in a year where he again rocked himself against the hollow wall, quietly moaning for the only person in the universe he had ever loved that deeply in his heart.

As you pull your baby boy to your shoulder, though, you check the pier house one more time for Michael, but see only Jessica hugging her friend Barbara, and Sarah holding Brendan, tears streaming down her face in joy and despair, the water rolling, as it always does, and crashing against the shore.

You know Michael could not be there, even if he had wanted to. He had actually remembered to call the night before and tell you matter-of-factly that he absolutely couldn't leave the August clinic . . . all scholarship players were obligated to attend. Practice. Doubles. No excuses.

Nevertheless, you look, the same way you once looked for Brenda each lonely morning.

And when you finally call Brenda again, in the middle of the night, just a week after the wedding, you cut her off as soon as she recognizes your voice and wails out your name. "You're dead to me, Brenda. You're dead to the children. Don't call. Don't write." And you drop the phone into the cradle.

Chapter 16

It is Wednesday, and that means nobody will be in *The Island Weekly* office all day: the typesetter, layout man, and reporter are off, and with Sarah and Brendan having moved to Chapel Hill, you will be alone in the van, delivering papers from Duck down to Hatteras Village.

You had left the cottage earlier than usual, before Jessica and Woody went to school, driving first over to the printer in Manteo, where you loaded the van and headed up to Donald's General Store in Duck. From there you drove south through shops in Kitty Hawk and Kill Devil Hills, and finally to an afternoon stop at Claire's Pit Barbecue in Nags Head. At each place there was a delivery and an important bit of small talk. At Claire's, you had shredded pork with slaw and a side of collards in a white Styrofoam bowl. If not a great day, it was a beautiful day.

By 3 p.m. you are speeding along the long strip of National Seashore on Pea Island, the van more than half empty, the west wind pushing and gusting, and you are, as usual, holding tightly on to the wheel, just managing to keep the tires to the right of the center line.

Although you have come to resent the hours these Wednesday deliveries take away from Jessica and the production of the newspaper, you still feel you can't afford another employee and, besides, you are usually able to turn some of the small talk into ads or free articles, both of which are indispensable to the survival of the paper.

This long drive going nowhere is also the only safe place for you to think about Brenda.

You still haven't told anyone anything about finding her, not even Jessica. For you, perhaps beyond your understanding, it is like spotting a fin just off the shore at the end of the day, knowing it would be best just to turn away and never think of it again rather than frightening everyone. There are sharks in the ocean, everybody knows that, and everybody knows they occasionally come near shore, but the mere mention of a fin would bring out terror on the beach for years . . . "She didn't even goddamn call me!" you growl, driving past the cream-colored brick Rangers' station, a blue heron in the reeds on the right.

"She didn't even goddamn call me," you repeat, as if there is someone in the van to be convinced, double-checking the rearview mirror, just to make sure that you are still alone. And when you see the soft slope of the cottage roofs way out in front, you roll down the window and bray, "Now she fucking calls the office every day and hangs up!" Your voice trails off. "I know it's her."

That Wednesday you make five stops in the three towns and are tempted to stop by the *Weekly* office just to sit for a moment by the phone, but, as usual, you're running late and have made arrangements to meet Jessica and Woody down in Buxton, so you just roll on.

At a little past 4 p.m., which you later realize would have been just about the time the University of North Carolina Dean Halloran's secretary was slipping a small brass key from the lock on her desk, you are leaving the Salvo Marina and heading toward Avon. And in the fall light on the National Seashore, you are deciding once again—as you had done the previous two weeks—that you are going to tell Jessica about Brenda. That night. If no one else, at least she should know.

Since that afternoon in August when a stranger named Sharon something disrupted whatever peace you had imagined was finally your own, you have felt as if you are cheating on your new wife, hiding something so profound—so much more adulterous than the brief affair you had had with Marlo all those lives ago—that you are sure it will poison your new marriage before long.

If I hadn't proposed so impulsively, you think, the whoosh of a big semi roaring in the opposite direction nearly blowing the van into a ditch, *then I certainly would've told her right away.* But after the proposal it seemed absolutely impossible to mention it without creating a mistrust in Jessica so deep that she would never stop doubting your sincerity.

Avon is right ahead.

No one at the grocery wants to talk.

At 4:30, you can see up ahead the black and white rings around the Hatteras lighthouse. The lead story in *The Weekly* this week is on the prediction of a geologist from UNC that the erosion around the structure is so rapid that the beacon will fall into the ocean by 1990, which feels like a million years, a million miles, a million lifetimes away.

Two hundred miles away, as you later find out, Dean Halloran, having waited through twenty-five rings with his heart thumping, puts the heavy phone back on the cradle.

You make two quick stops along the strip in Buxton—The Channel Bass Grocery and Sawyer's Bait and Tackle—and then drive straight down to the Cape Hatteras School. Woody and Jessica are up on the warm hood of her beat-up green Chevy Impala. They wave, exaggerating their excitement, as you pull into the bus circle, the van bouncing in a deep pothole causing a stack of papers to slide across the plywood floor.

Even though the one-story brick building is only twelve years old, the metal doors and casings around the windows are bubbling badly with rust. That rust is something that you've never gotten used to on the island after all this time, that relentless destruction by the salty air. You quickly turn your gaze and your thoughts to the two of them sliding off the hood.

As had quickly become the custom on Wednesdays that fall, Jessica jumps into the front captain's seat—

"where Mom sat," Woody told her once—and Woody sits between the bundles of papers on the rear bench.

The first thing they say to you, shouting over the road noise after you get back on Highway 12, is that they had just been talking about Woody going to Chapel Hill for a weekend to see Sarah.

"And Michael, too," Woody adds, not wanting Jessica or you to think he doesn't care about his brother.

You can already feel that there's another shoe to drop, but have no idea what it is other than that it involves Chapel Hill. You shrug it away and drive off to complete deliveries in Buxton, Frisco, Hatteras Village, and finally on to the Ocracoke ferry, where Earl Mann signs for the final two bundles.

After that, as always, you go to the Soft Shell Drive-In and have crab-cake sandwiches, hush puppies, and the best homemade coleslaw on the Banks, everybody oohing and aahing as if they've never tasted any of it before.

And on the forty-five-minute ride back to Rodanthe in the dark empty van, you retreat into your private self. The night is cool and you turn on the heat for the first time this year.

You are still thinking about Brenda, feeling the same nauseating emptiness that has been twisting your stomach for three years. It no longer matters whether you are thinking that she's dead, or run away, or even making love to another man—or, now, simply thinking about telling Jessica that she is still alive. There's no satisfying answer. So you decide—as you had decided the days before—to tell Jessica the truth as soon as you get back to the cottage. After Woody is asleep.

Now Woody turns sideways and leans back on the ripped armrest of the bench seat and starts talking, first in a low mumble and then louder over the rumble of the engine, the high whine of the tires, and the wind, wondering what you think of his idea of moving in with Sarah next summer, and then staying with her for the school year.

You can see that the second part is news to Jessica. And it so surprises the hell out of you—a sting and an ache like a needle in the heart of a muscle—that you just keep driving, nodding affably like Woody, who is now trying to explain in adult terms why he no longer wants to be on the island. He says he is tired of walking the beach with nowhere to go, tired of feeling like a tagalong despite—and maybe because of—your attempts to include him in practically everything you and Jessica do. "Everyone has gone," he says.

In the whining darkness of the van slicing through the blowing barrier-island sands, a squall moving south over Pea Island toward Rodanthe, Woody builds his case for moving: better schools, more opportunity to meet different people, gaining independence—all the things a fourteen-year-old might think an adult wants to hear. He organizes it like the five-paragraph essay he was taught to write at school by Mr. Clark.

In Salvo, you turn on the big windshield wipers after a few sprinkles and glance over at Jessica for something, anything, to undermine Woody's arguments, but Jessica seems as oblivious to Woody's logic as she is to the change in the weather, lost in some rhapsody that you will not learn for days.

It is raining hard by the time you get back to Caminada Bay and trudge up the wooden stairs, all three of you bending your necks away from the sheets of gusting water. When you hear the phone ringing in the cottage, Woody leaps up the remaining steps, pushes open the door, and races across the dark room to the phone.

By the time he snatches the receiver off the cradle, though, whoever was on the line has already hung up. He says, "It must have been Sarah."

* * *

Woody is already reading in bed when Dean Halloran calls again fifteen minutes later. And fifteen minutes after that life-altering call, you are driving into some dark and cold future, hands tight on the steering wheel, red eyes staring straight ahead through the sweeping rain and the reflective sweep of the wipers back and forth, back and forth, across the large windshield.

The few oncoming headlights blur whatever visibility you can muster, swerving onto the sand shoulders, pumping the brakes, but once you are past the lights in Manteo, you rarely lift your foot from the accelerator, moving with the force of the wind toward Chapel Hill, the Southern Part of Heaven, and your poor dead child.

* * *

A security guard lets you inside the Carr Building with a sad, knowing nod. The Dean is waiting for you, alone in his warmly appointed office, tie loosened and his sleeves rolled up, sleepy, distraught, then agitated when you demand information that only Michael could have provided—and probably not even Michael, whose emptiness apparently knew no logic. "How could this have happened?" you shout at a man whose job is deflecting shouts all day long.

"I don't know, Mr. Hudson." He shakes his head. "I am truly sorry I can't help you any more than this. As much as I have found out, Michael never said anything to his roommate. He didn't even leave a note. As I believe I said, Jim Fenster, his roommate, thought it had something to do with a girl, a girl named Annabel, but we don't know much more than that. I am so sorry."

You drop your face in your hands and weep. There is nothing else to do.

Then there are the formalities: the excruciating, stark truth of the mandatory identification over at the University Hospital morgue—the cold look on Michael's smooth face, an aching reminder of the blank stares across the kitchen table, the pockmark on his nose making you wail, making you turn away from your son and the pathologist who holds the sheet.

Then there are documents to be signed in the overheated office. Arrangements to be made to have his body transferred to Hatteras. The awkward meeting with Jim Fenster, Michael's roommate, who ignorantly and arrogantly takes a measure of responsibility for the suicide.

Fenster is in his pajamas. "I'm so sorry, Mr. Hudson," he cries, his flat, freckled, unshaven face in his trembling hands. "I'm so sorry . . . I shoulda been able to do something, sir. Michael talked about her one night, but I didn't know what to say."

Chapter 17

"You know," the Dean says confidentially to you, "they all considered Michael just a naive kid from Hatteras who knew little about life except how to put the ball in the hoop. Mr. Klinghoffer even told me that Michael grew up on the Outer Banks and had never been off the islands until he came here . . . and from all I gathered, Mr. Hudson, I don't think Michael ever told them anything about where he'd been or what he'd seen. Or . . ." His voice trails off to nothing.

As far as he knows, Annabel is not a bad person. Or even a "bad influence," as Michael's buddies had apparently told Mr. Evans over at Security, just before you spoke to Dean Halloran.

Best you can figure she was just a young girl. Too young to see the desperation behind the freshman basketball player's sometimes gawky gestures, or the meaning behind his long silences, or his refusal to talk about his family.

You learn that Annabel is all of nineteen, a sophomore English major from Asheville, a Tri Delta who wanted no more—and no less—than to have the best four years of her life in Chapel Hill. She simply liked the tall, athletic Michael when he was being sweet, and then when he grew morose, she didn't. That's all.

You get that.

It was when he woke up for classes that Jim Fenster found Michael fully clothed and on his back early that morning, his left arm dangling to the floor, four empty bottles of aspirin and a half drunk fifth of Southern Comfort on the bed. He said Michael didn't move when he poked him with a finger on his shoulder—or a hushed minute later when he prodded him again—and then Jim stumbled hysterically out into the empty hall to bang his fists on the door of the Resident Advisor, Charles Teeter.

From what you piece together, from all the ragged stories you hear first- and second- and thirdhand, Charles Teeter came racing into the room in his undershorts, shook Michael's cold body, felt his neck for a pulse, put his ear to Michael's waxy mouth to feel if there was any breath, and began doing the CPR which he had just learned that summer, yelling between compressions for someone to call Campus Security. Security immediately radioed for the Chapel Hill Rescue Squad. And no more than three minutes later, the paramedics continued the resuscitation Teeter had begun, but Michael was long since cold, blood pooling in his extremities.

When you realize that the sound you hear is Jim Fenster bawling "I'm sorry, I'm sorry, I'm sorry," snot running down over his lips and glistening on his chin, you go sit down next to him, put your arm around his thin shoulders, tell him in a voice that doesn't sound like yours that it's not his fault, that "my son was more unhappy than you'll ever know." And with that you pat him on his bent back, lean over, and kiss his head.

Michael's bags are packed on the bare mattress. You get up without another word, pick up the bags, carry them out of the room and over to the elevator. When you press the down button, you realize that there is still a duffel bag left in the room, but you can't bear to go back, pushing the lighted button again and going down to the lobby and out to the parking lot without another moment's reflection.

You toss the suitcases into the van and drive off the familiar campus and over to Carrboro to see Sarah, who still knows nothing about her brother. You hadn't had the strength to call her before you saw the Dean, praying that it would all be a mistake. Someone else's son.

* * *

At an all-night 7-11 on the edge of the two towns, you spy an unlit phone booth and suddenly swing the van into the gravelly lot, skidding to a halt. As you push a slippery dime into the slot, you notice the orange sky over an apartment complex, and dial a zero and the number you had memorized the first time you heard it in August.

A cheery operator's voice crackles through the receiver, and you tell her in a monotone to reverse the charges. You give your full name as the phone begins to ring.

"Yes?" A groggy voice agrees to the charges. "Yes. Peter?"

It takes you a few seconds to clear the phlegm clogging your throat. "Brenda," you start and stop.

"Oh! Oh, Peter, it's you. I thought you'd never get back . . . I was so afraid . . . did you get my letter?"

You hear some rustling and the snap of a match.

"Brenda, I am not calling—"

"No, I know," she quickly cuts you off. "I'm not expecting anything. I just thought that I'd never hear from you again after I mailed that letter." She is hyperventilating. "I know you don't—"

"You don't know anything," you slice through viciously. "You don't know one fucking thing!"

"I know."

"No, you don't know anything." You are blubbering now. "You don't know a goddamn fucking thing. Michael's dead!" You hear her gasp. "That's what you don't fuckin' know! He killed himself, and it's all your fucking fault. It's all your fucking fault!!"

Brenda is wailing so loudly now that you scream at her to shut up, and when you look around the empty parking lot you see a girl in a hairnet behind the 7-11 counter glaring through the window, but you don't care anymore, you show her your twisted face and scream even louder, "You don't know anything! YOU DON'T KNOW SHIT!!"

Now it's you who is heaving with sobs, drowning out the cries of hysteria on the other end, a man's voice in the background yelling at her to calm down, but you are not done. "ONE FUCKING THING!" you bellow, then hold the phone flush to your shaking gut, trying to stop the flood of sobs, wiping your nose on your wrist and biting your lower lip until you taste blood mixing with the snot.

After a while, deep tremulous breaths tucked away into your chest, you put the receiver back to your ear and hear her sobs. You open your thick, wet mouth, but there is nothing more to say. "You just don't know anything," you scratch out in a whisper and then drop the black phone, leaving it dangling on the long cord, banging around senselessly against the plexiglass side.

You don't actually remember driving over to Sarah's place, but once you find yourself in the dusty hall you recognize Brendan's giggle and Sarah's baby talk.

Sarah is just putting a spoon into Brendan's mouth when you walk through the unlocked door. She looks over at you, and you know she mirrors your horror.

And you know that what you tell her cannot be any less painful than if she had actually seen Michael take each pill, one by one.

When the baby cries out for more food, Sarah pushes herself away from your arms and you smell the intense odor of your own panic. Her face is wet and utterly blank. She holds her hands to her side and turns her palms your way. The spoon is between her thumb and forefinger.

In the lull, Brendan wails again, banging the tray of his high chair with his fat hand and arching his back. So you take the spoon and tell Sarah to pack some things for the baby and herself. She starts to protest, but obviously doesn't know why.

Brendan quiets down as soon as you scoop up some of the oatmeal and lay the shaking spoon on his tongue. *My grandchild*, you think, as if understanding your relationship for the first time as you feed this little boy in his yellow Dr. Dentons opening his pink mouth for each spoonful until the white ceramic bowl with bunnies is scraped clean.

You wipe the baby's mouth and pull him up out of the high chair, pressing your rough face against his smooth cheeks, sniffing deeply as you begin to weep and Brendan giggles.

* * *

During the sunny ride back to Hatteras, Brendan seems very happy, chattering and singing on the bench seat with his red-faced mother, watching the bright world zoom by in the big side windows of the van.

You and Sarah speak only once during the entire five-and-a-half-hour drive, not only because of the rusted muffler and the whine of the underinflated tires, but because there's nothing to say.

"I should have called last night!" Sarah finally blurts out somewhere around Rocky Mount, but you can't make out what she's saying. So when she leans forward and repeats herself, more loudly this time, "If only I called last night!" you find her in the rearview mirror and holler, "Don't you dare!" pointing savagely at her reflection. "That boy died three and a half years ago!" you yell over the engine rumble.

The baby looks up at the sound of your booming voice, but Sarah does not move, eyes wide, tears running down her cheeks; the rumble of the engine, the road noise, the static inside your head.

Brendan soon falls asleep, then wakes as you roll through quiet

Mann's Harbor, then sucks on a warm bottle of apple juice as you drive across the two bridges and the unseasonably hot barrier two lane toward the cottage that Brenda Hudson had once refused to leave.

* * *

When you get back to Caminada Bay, Jessica runs out to hug Sarah and take Brendan out of his car seat. She envelops the boy in her arms, his head on her breast, her cheek on his warm head. She tells you that she made all the local arrangements early that morning before Woody awoke. Called the Midgett Funeral Home in Manteo and arranged for the minister at the Rodanthe Presbyterian Church to take care of the service.

When Sarah takes the baby and goes inside to change his diaper, Jessica tells you that when Woody wandered bleary-eyed out of his room to get ready for school earlier in the morning, she had put her arms around his thin shoulders and asked him to sit on the sofa with her. She says he looked frail and confused in his pale-yellow pajamas as they sank together into the cushions. She smoothed the shock of hair off his forehead. "Your dad, he went to Chapel Hill . . ."

After she was finished, Woody opened his brown eyes very wide and said, "He's dead?" in a soft, high voice.

She nodded and pulled him close before he could say or do anything. He allowed her to hold him and rock him, the heat of his breath on her shoulder.

After a while, he arched his back away from her.

"I'm sorry, Woody," she says she said. "I know how you must feel."

His expression was blank. "He's really dead? He's not sick or something?" he said, shaking his head the way his sister used to do.

"I told him that he didn't have to go to school today. I told him that I was going to stay home all day. I asked if maybe he'd like to go to Covington's house later. He just shrugged."

Chapter 18

Jessica is behind you as you climb the steps and head directly to Woody's room, glancing back to make sure she's still there. She points and you nod, knock, then wait until Woody emerges, head lowered. There are tears, your arms around his thin shoulders, but no words.

At least until Sarah, tears slipping down her red cheeks, asks Woody to please take Brendan for a walk. He shrugs and walks out the screen door followed by the three adults, down the steps to the driveway, where he waits patiently for Sarah to ease Brendan into the rusty umbrella stroller.

The three of you stand there watching him push the little boy up the bumpy road past the small gray motel cottages.

When he is out of sight, Jessica tells you that Woody spent the cool morning alone in his bedroom, working on an F-16 model fighter plane that he and Covington were building together on Saturdays.

She checked on him every so often, watching from the hall as he fiddled with the minute gray plastic parts, trying to piece it all together and get it glued before his dad returned to the cottage. He'd look up at her, then down again as if her red eyes and swollen nose were annoying him.

* * *

You are standing on the lower deck when the boys return. There are already two cars parked off the side of the narrow beach road.

Woody walks past Nancy Sawyer's Pinto, but stops in front of the rusted Volkswagen. He peers into the passenger window. You think to call out something funny to your boy, but can't find the strength, so you turn around and walk back inside.

Moments later Woody enters the cottage carrying Brendan on his hip. Nancy Sawyer is leaning on the sink and smoking. You and Jessica have your arms around each other like young lovers, but you are merely holding each other up.

Woody's eyes scan the small living room. You know he's looking for the owner of the VW.

Rin Wabash is in the overstuffed chair in the corner talking to Sarah, who is sitting sideways on the couch, opening her arms for the baby. Woody looks somewhat skeptically over at the strange man-boy, and Sarah quickly introduces him as a friend from Chapel Hill, "Brendan's best buddy."

Rin explains how he had looked for Brendan early that morning—he was supposed to babysit until his 11 a.m. economics class—and had finally tracked them down through Andrea, the hostess at the restaurant where Sarah worked. When Andrea told him about Michael, he left Chapel Hill right away and drove straight to 64 East, past one dusty Piedmont town after another, across Alligator River and then onto Roanoke Island, following the twisted signs across the drawbridge to Nags Head where, as the only car on the two lane, he signaled right onto Highway 12 and soon found himself climbing the Herbert Bonner Bridge and looking out at the most beautiful sight he'd ever seen . . . a green ocean breaking just beyond the white Coast Guard Station. He had never seen the ocean before. Fourteen miles of National Seashore later, he drove right through Rodanthe and then Waves and Salvo, and at the Salvo Market and Marina someone told him he'd passed the Hudsons' road three miles back.

It is clear to everyone in the room that Woody has taken an

instant dislike to Rin, who smiles his broadest country-boy smile and looks like he's about to say something guaranteed to charm his girlfriend's little brother when everyone turns to a rustling by the screen door.

It is Covington's mother, big as a loggerhead, framed in the doorway. She smiles politely and lets herself in, walks directly over to Woody, and holds him in her heavy white arms. He offers no resistance when she pulls his head down on her large breasts. "You poor baby," she whispers. "Come with me," she says, and leads him over to you, still standing in the kitchen. She hugs you, whispering, "I'm gonna take Woody home with me. It'll probably be good for him to get away from all this for a while. Covington'll be home soon."

When she steps back from the one-sided embrace, you just stand there, staring numbly over her shoulder into space. Jessica touches her elbow, offering thanks and telling her that the service will be the next morning at eleven, pointing to the brick church behind the cottage.

* * *

There is a breeze rustling the pages in old Reverend Covey's black book. Behind him, you stare at the graves leaning out of the sand like they had grown tired of the wind constantly blowing over them, howling like a hammer. The reverend looks all around at the small congregation, some in Sunday suits, some in bathing suits, waits until everyone is looking at him, and says: "Job 7:13-15: My bed shall comfort me, my couch shall ease my complaint; Then thou scarest me with dreams, and terrifiest me through visions; So that my soul chooseth strangling, and death rather than life."

You want to howl, you want to scream out that Michael didn't hang himself. *How cruel!* you think, staring right into the reverend's mouth, his tongue wagging senselessly inside. You look to the side at Woody to see if he is all right. He is standing there listlessly between you and Jessica, leaning on neither. Mrs. Parker is behind him, her thick pink hand on his shoulder.

Now the old reverend, who has never met Michael, but certainly knows about the blind and ignorant ways people live their lives, is quoting from Corinthians: "We are perplexed, but not in despair."

And you suddenly understand then, as if it had been written in your soul all along, that despair comes only from arrogant assumptions about the way things should be. And out of nowhere, the heavens it seems, you gain a tenuous grasp of everything (*every goddamn thing!*) that has perplexed you all your life . . . not just why Brenda left you or why you assumed she never would, but why you have never felt safe anywhere. "The wind bloweth where it listeth, and thou heareth the sound thereof, but canst not tell whence it cometh and whither it goeth: so is everyone that is born of the Spirit."

Then there is the usual—oddly comforting—"Yea though I walk through the valley . . ." followed by the awful sound of the crank used to lower the coffin into the damp hole squeaking with each rotation as the reverend crosses himself and mumbles something.

You turn away from the hole as the box comes even with the sandy ground, glancing back behind you at the large solemn crowd staring beyond you. Practically the entire Cape Hatteras School is standing on the damp ground, the girls weeping, the boys' eyes like wet concrete. Michael's teachers are there, heads down, hands clasped behind their backs.

Way in the back, behind a wall of weeping, mismatched Cape Hatteras School boys and girls, some dressed for church, some for the beach, you catch sight of a woman mostly obscured by the wide shoulders of Elvin Midgett, a woman in black, a black veil covering her downturned face, and the blood drains from your head. Pools in your belly.

You see that Sarah sees her, too, and that her mouth is open in an "o," and then she is dropping the baby bottle in the sand and grabbing Jessica's hand like she is going to collapse, the baby dangling from her other arm.

From behind, Rin grabs her shoulders as she falls to her knees and Jessica scoops up the baby.

And moments later, when you find yourself kneeling, holding Sarah close to your chest, you feel Brenda in the sobs. And when she whispers, "I saw her! I saw her! Her ghost, Dad, her ghost!" you know exactly what she has seen, turning and angrily scanning the crowd for the face that you know is there; the face you knew would be there the moment you saw her in the distance.

But you see nothing, nothing but a sea of dark eyes staring your way. No one skulking behind those goodhearted mourners. No one walking away toward the road.

So when you look to the blue sky to curse Brenda and God himself, the sun shocks your eyes, the whole world spins in orange and red circles, and you see another woman, hidden behind a veil so sad the waters are stilled and the sky is bleached white . . . she is carrying Michael in her arms. She is walking on top of the shallow Sound, the sun sparkling all around, her tears falling like kaleidoscopic rain onto glass. And when she turns to look at you, calling your name, your knees buckle. "Mr. Hudson," the minister says perhaps a little too sharply, and you shake away the vision, and the only thing you see is a gnarly finger pointed at the shovel full of sand.

So you pick it up, sand spilling over the rusted edges, and heave it into the hole, shovel and sand falling the four feet into the earth, landing with a dull thud on the polished surface of the casket.

Then you lead your children away from this gash in the island, as much holding them as pushing, your hands on their narrow shoulders all the way back to the van.

And when you think they're all settled in their seats, Sarah next to you in the ripped captain's chair, Woody on the bench behind, you pull the heavy driver's door closed, reach for the ignition, and hear the engine roar to life, when Woody cries out, "Wait for Jessica and Brendan!"

Startled and confused, a fury rising in you like a water spout, you slam the heel of your hand on the wheel, the engine racing.

Sarah leans across into the eye of your storm and says, "I thought I saw her. I really thought I saw her. Her ghost? That's what happened."

"I know," you whisper back. You turn your head so that you're almost nose to nose. "Maybe you did," you say, and the confusion in her eyes turns to horror.

You want to reach out for her hand then, but instead tighten your hold on the steering wheel. "No," you say out loud, shaking your head, "I didn't mean that. Just that sometimes I see her, too."

"Who?" says Woody from behind. His voice is cracking. "Who do you see?"

You turn to your boy and see the face of your own betrayal, your own hope. "Mother Mary," you say. "I think sometimes we see what we want to see."

Then Mrs. Parker is tapping you on the shoulder, standing at the open window, asking if it's all right to take Woody with her. You nod as Jessica passes Brendan through the open window on the other side to his mother. And Jessica pulls herself up through the double rusting doors of the van, as Woody jumps out and runs over to the brand-new shiny Ford Fairmont.

* * *

By the time you get back to the cottage, there are already a few cars parked outside. Inside, a chattering group of women from the Rodanthe Community Center are fixing platters and drinks for the people who will be stopping by all afternoon.

When Sarah jumps down onto the driveway with Brendan on her hip, you turn to Jessica and say, "I don't know whether I can face them all."

Jessica's hoarse voice rises above the rumbling engine. "They're just tryin' to help."

You rub your eyes with aching fingers, pushing and poking behind the occipital bone. "Well, I'm afraid no one can help me right now."

The two of you sit in the idling van, waiting.

After a while, you mumble an apology and say you're still not ready to face anyone. Jessica nods and you shut off the ignition, shoulder the rusted door open, wander across the road, stopping momentarily to remove your tie and jacket, and walk back to the van to toss them through the window.

As you climb the dune you hear more cars pulling up to the cottage. Then you're over the top, sliding down through the soft sand on the ocean side, laboring with each step toward the water.

Once you reach the hard sand you lengthen your stride and head north, reminded with each step of the day you and the kids spent on the beach searching for Brenda. How Woody came racing over the dunes screaming that he'd seen her. You can still taste the metal in your mouth.

This time is different, though. This time you know she is there. Somewhere. Maybe on the pier. And this time you are going to find her and you are going to kill her before she does any more damage.

As you approach the massive crossed pilings, you are pointing your finger menacingly, telling her that she should be in the casket, not Michael; that she'd been dead for three years already; that she didn't know one fucking thing. "NOTHING!!!!!!!!!!!!" you roar from the empty beach out into the mindless crashing waves.

And when you finally climb up on the long, rickety pier, you imagine grabbing her, lifting her in your arms, holding her briefly up over your head, and heaving her over the rail, her arms and legs like a startled mannequin as she drops the thirty-five feet to the whipped-up ocean below, pounded unconscious against the rugged pilings, slipping lifelessly, invisibly, beneath the surf.

Forever.

Brenda is not on the pier, though. No one there but a few of the ol' boys jawing about this and that. They stop talking when they see you coming. Out of the corner of a blurred eye you think you see Brenda walking up the beach, but when the figure in black gets closer, you see that it's just Dana Covey, still in her funeral dress.

You can feel the frosty gaze of the fishermen on your back as you retrace your steps back to the pier house, down the steps to the sand, and begin racing north up the beach, racing across the slanted hard sand until you are nearly a mile up the deserted strand and a big swell sweeps up over your dancing steps, soaking your black shoes and socks and the cuffs of your suit slacks. Then you are bellowing obscenities, chest heaving, fist raised at the blue horizon, throat on fire until your yowling is drowned out in the unending roar of the surf.

You fall to the wet sand, pluck off your shoes, stand up and toss one and then the other over the next breakers, now screaming "Fuck Youuuuuuu!!! FUUUUCK . . . YOUUUUUUUUU!!!!!!!"

Your legs like overstretched coils, your brain full of hammers, you turn on your heels and stagger toward the dune, falling backwards into the shallow cave formed by the last nor'easter, wild roots of sea oats pressing your white shirt soaked with sweat.

Now there is nothing left in your world but the whoosh of your breath, your chest rising and falling, your heart thudding, until you hear a voice from behind say, "Peter . . ."

You don't have to turn. Don't want to turn. The oddest thing is that after all that rage you are relieved to hear that voice, finally.

Your clenched palm opens, cool dry sand slips through the humid air, scattering into the grainy earth beneath you, your palms turned and pressing down, heart ticking, the unstoppable wind another tremulous breath before the next crashing wave.

"Peter . . . ," she says again. The cottony voice is above you, behind you, somewhere in the sea oats. You refuse to turn around.

"You know," you say finally, speaking to the ocean, "I would have killed you, tossed you right over the end of the pier."

"I know," she says so calmly. "And I would have deserved it. That's why I didn't follow you up there. I'm a coward. I waited."

"For what?"

"For you."

"I didn't want you to come. Why did you come?"

"Because it's all my fault. Everything. I had to come here. I had to face it. I had to tell you."

"I don't want to hear it."

"I know."

"I can never forgive you."

"I know."

"You can't see the children."

"I know . . . I know."

Then there is just the wind barely whistling. You don't raise your voice now. "You don't know anything, Brenda. You don't know one fucking thing."

She doesn't reply, but from behind you, you hear some shifting in the dune, then feel a hand brushing your arm, a soft weight on your shoulder, warm breath on your bare neck. "I'm so sorry, my love."

"It's all your fault," you weep.

"Yesssss."

Then there is the wind. Again. Always the wind. Now you are whispering, her dry lips on your neck. "Don't think I don't know it's not all your fault." The water falls from your eyes as you weep for all the blind universe to see.

Out in the distance you see an enormous ray flip over. And a moment later, you realize she is gone.

A moment after that, you do not know whether she was ever there.

CHAPTER 19

RODANTHE, NC, APRIL 1976

At 6 a.m. you begin your wakeful day in much the same manner as you have begun nearly every morning for the past four years. You open your eyes, focusing first on the mirror over the dresser until you can see the window clearly, and then, as before, as always, a private meditation in which you identify for yourself alone the point in time where this life has taken you—where you are, where the living children are, and more recently, to whom you are married—and then slide silently out from beneath the warm sheet into the cool sticky air, focused only on locating shorts and sneakers, unaware that Jessica is watching from the rumpled other side of the bed.

"And where ya goin', handsome?"

Startled, you look back at the pregnant goddess through the mirror. "Hey."

She does look beautiful, voluptuous, full of life. "It's just past six, what are you doing up?"

"I think I'm finished sleeping for the next few months." She pats her belly and smiles sadly. "If it's not my back or heartburn or trying to get comfortable with this watermelon in my belly, I have to pee every two hours."

You laugh, maybe a little too mechanically, thinking you've heard all that—and more—before from a different voice, and then step into a crumpled, cold jock, straightening the straps around your cheeks with a hop. "That's not so bad," you say thoughtlessly. "You can get used to not sleeping. I don't think I've had a deep sleep in three or four years."

You see her wince. "I'm sorry," you say.

She nods, her graceful hands swirling around that massive belly. "But I have to say you seemed pretty dead to the world at five. . . ," she says, tilting her head and smiling a full smile as you step into Michael's blue Cape Hatteras gym shorts.

"I was faking," you say with a grin, poking through the open drawer for a T-shirt. "Did you do any laundry?"

"No, I've given up bending down." Then another smile, a squiggly one this time. "Why don't you just take off all those silly things and make love to your wife and baby?"

You can feel your eyebrows rising against your will, blood coming and going from your extremities. "Oooooh, now that is tempting, but . . . nope . . . nope—gotta run, sweetheart. Gotta run. Places to go. People to . . . y'know."

"No, I don't know," she says.

You press your lips together. "I'm sorry, Jess. I just don't know how to get going if I don't just get going."

She holds one hand, fingers bent, on her breast; the other is in the air gesturing you back to the warm bed, a devilish smirk informing her rounded face. "I'm pretty sure I can get you going."

But, tempting as she is—and she is all that—you have to go. You really have to go. "Later," you say to the mirror and, trying to be funny, yank yourself by the ear out of the small bedroom, sneakers in one hand, a smelly white Rosslyn High School Boosters T-shirt in the other.

"You don't know what you're missing, sailor!" she yells after you.

"Oh yes I do . . . it'll make me run faster," you call back over your shoulder, turning out of the narrow hall into the recarpeted living room, past the new couch and out onto the deck.

* * *

When you pad through the open door an hour or more later, white towel around your waist, you're surprised to still see Jessica in bed. When she sees you, she pulls the sheet over her breasts.

"You haven't moved," you say, suddenly stirring, glancing in the mirror and pushing your wet hair straight back.

"It's Saturday; I'm not movin' one lick. What are you gonna do?"

You drop the towel. "What am I gonna do? Well, first I'm going to make love to my gorgeous wife . . ."

You wait for a sign, but she just lies there wide eyed, her hand spinning at the wrist. "And . . . ?"

"Well," you say, bending down to pick up the towel, "I'm going to ride off to the Pulitzer Prize–winning *Island Weekly* like I do eight days a week—and then, don't you remember?—I'm going over to Portsmouth Island to do the story on the Park Service leasing the houses there to anyone who'll renovate them."

"Oh right! You did tell me, I just forgot. But I wish you'd stay home with me, Peter. Let's spend the day in bed, just foolin' around and talking. I've got a few things on my mind . . . and a couple tricks up my sleeve." She winks.

Confused, you smile and sit down on the soft bed. "How about if I stick around for breakfast," you say, leaning over to kiss her belly through the sheets. "Then I really gotta go. I'll be back on Tuesday."

She shakes her head. Looks like she might cry. "The story can wait, can't it?"

Now it's your turn to do some head shaking. But Jessica seems undeterred. "I mean, it's Portsmouth Island. Nothing's happened there in a hundred years. Nothing's likely to happen if you wait a week."

"Wrong again, Carnac," you say, trying to avoid the coming squall. "First, I gotta get to Portsmouth now, before you get much further along. I don't want to be stuck over there when you go into labor."

"Yeah, and?" The spinning hand again.

"And I gotta go to the office because the bigger this island gets, the more meetings these people think of making up. And they get mad and cancel ads if I don't write them up. Sometimes I think I'm nothing more than a delivery boy of gossip and misinformation. They don't listen to each other at all in their meetings, and they sure as hell don't seem to read the articles except to check if their names are spelled right."

"So let's go," she blurts out, out of nowhere it seems. "Let's just the two of us get out of here."

"I am going," you say. "I've gotta be down in Hatteras Village by ten to get the boat. And you're in no condition to travel to that mosquito-infested place."

"No," she says, putting her hand on yours. "I mean let's get out of here. Let's get off this island."

A cool breeze passes over the bed and blows some papers off the bureau. You take your hand back. "What are you talking about?" You can hear your voice rising like it's a kite over the breakers.

She is nodding before any words come out of her thick-as-summer mouth. "I think I want to move out of here, Peter—this cottage, the island."

"Jessica, what are you talking about? You're gonna have a baby in two months."

"Peter," she says, grabbing your hand and pressing the palm down on her belly, "are you happy here? Are you really happy?"

"I don't know," you say, wary of any trap you might be stepping into. "I'm happy with you, happier than I've ever been in my life. I love you. Honestly, I haven't even thought about leaving this island in a very long time. This is just where I live, where I work. What are you talking about? Where did all this come from?"

"I'm sorry I didn't choose a better time to bring all this up, but I've had a lot of time to sit around and think about our lives . . . our future."

And you realize in that moment that, like a line cast out over the breakers, there is no way to call it back until it sinks beneath the surface.

"Peter, this island," she begins, "is full of bad memories. It's full of death for both of us. That's why we lived here for so long. Let's start all over again someplace new—for the baby. Maybe we could go to Chapel Hill with Woody and Sarah and Brendan and Rin? We could all live together. Maybe we could—" Her eyes are wide open and glassy.

"Jesus Christ, Jessica, I told you this was gonna happen someday!" You hadn't; you just imagined that you must have told her sometime. Your mouth is full of metal. Again.

Jessica rolls over on her side to sit up and, having lost the sheet, pulls it back up over her full breasts. "You've told me lots of times that you'd never have stayed here except for Brenda or the kids."

"Right."

"Well, sorry to be so blunt, but Brenda's dead, Peter. And so is Michael." She visibly shudders as she says it. "You know, practically every other kid in his twelfth-grade class is planning to leave the island as soon as graduation comes—Woody couldn't even wait that long."

"That was different."

"Maybe, but not really. Peter, this is a wonderful place to go on vacation, or to run away from your life, but we have too much bad history here." She starts to cry. "It's so lonely, and it never feels like home."

You conjure up a sharp hook caught in your cheek, blood coating your tongue. "I gotta get out of here, Jessica," you say, pushing yourself up off the soft bed and starting to dress. "I don't know whether I can do this all again."

Now jamming your feet through the trousers, you grab a shirt out of the closet. A hanger springs off and bounces to the carpet.

Jessica catches your eye in the mirror. Her voice is a pitch too high—an eight-pound test line being tugged out. "You could sell the paper and we could go to Raleigh or Chapel Hill. Be with Sarah and Woody. There are lots of agencies that would die to have you."

You sit back down on the far edge of the bed and tug the socks over your damp feet.

"Peter . . . ," she says, but you won't turn her way. "Peter, I could teach there. Easily. We could get a real house . . ."

You step around the bed, looking down at the floor. When you find your docksiders, you step into them without a word and walk out of the room.

"Please don't!" she cries out, but you wave her back from behind, imagining her catching a last glimpse of your white shirt as you turn the corner into the living room.

The stairs rumble as you rush down to the sand. And although you thought you were headed toward the van and then to the office, you find yourself stomping across the empty lane, passing the salt-treated eight-by-eights in place for a new cottage on the ocean side, then striding up over the dunes, one hand thrown down as if you are arguing with Jessica. Still arguing with Brenda about where it all started. Heaving her over the pier. Still talking to her as if she sits behind you, never turning around.

All you intend to do is climb up through the grasses and over the dunes and beyond Jessica's sight. You're almost sure she's watching from the bedroom window.

Chest heaving up and down, you drop yourself into the sand and pull a wavering sea oat to your cheek as if it contains some mournful reminiscence, recalling the made-up and re-made-up memories of those lost summer days on the beach, a few weeks away from everything, Michael and Sarah bobbing in the surf, Woody piling sand on your outstretched feet, Brenda walking back from the water in her black bathing suit, dripping, glistening. That was the life. Your life.

You look down at your slacks and docksiders, trying to remember the last time that you spent the whole day on the beach. It has to have been more than a year. Easily more than a year.

Still sitting in the sand, you pivot to the side and glance into the waving sea oats behind you. Although the dune obscures everything but the threatening sky, you conjure up the small cottage, the rusted van in the driveway, the rip in the screen door, Jessica staring out the bedroom window, your baby inside of her.

And suddenly you know she will leave you, too, as surely as the waves pound the beach. You see the empty cottage in your mind and a chill grabs you in the hollow of your chest. A hard wind brings tears to your eyes as you fall back into the dune, the figure of a man way off in the misty distance walking toward the end of the pier and disappearing into the fog.

With the wind now whipping sand on your cheek and bare arm, you don't hear Jessica approaching, but as she steps heavily down the worn path to the beach, you hear the squish of bare feet in the sand and for reasons you can't explain to yourself, you know it's Jessica. It is not Brenda. And so you know in that instant that you will go to Chapel Hill or Raleigh or San Francisco or wherever she yearns to go. Anywhere.

You won't go for her, though—or anyone else. It would only be for you. It would be your decision. Your salvation. The wind is cold and the days too confusingly long to be without her. If you are a fool for love, then so be it. In this moment there is no one else for you on this earth. You have seen God on the beach, but it isn't any God you've ever seen before. You know now that you are going to be with Jessica forever.

Then her hard belly is on your back, her cool arms encircling your chest. Her hands are trembling.

Part IV

Portsmouth Island, NC, April 1976

CHAPTER 20

Even when the two of you are finally out on choppy Pamlico Sound in his twenty-one-foot whaler with a brand new Johnson, Raymond Sawyer never says a word. Never asks why you're heading out to Portsmouth.

Sawyer was never one for idle talking. Which is a good thing; you aren't talkative anyway, still wondering about Jessica and what is going to come of your life—and, more immediately, how you are going to survive the next two days.

So you fill your mind with the book you were reading back in Rodanthe: in 1860, Portsmouth Island was a thriving port town with nearly seven hundred residents. But with a hurricane opening up access to Ocracoke and Hatteras, Portsmouth's merchant trade quickly waned, and by the late forties it was practically deserted.

The Park Service, which then took over the island and the whole Cape Lookout National Seashore, began offering the abandoned houses and shops to anyone who would agree to maintain the properties.

And by 1976 there were several individuals, hermits you might say, who were willing to brave the muscular mosquitos and the harsh isolation in order to live quietly and simply with the terns, pipers, skimmers, oyster catchers, herons, and pelicans that call Portsmouth home.

Sawyer brings you up onto the empty beach and points across the dunes toward the Rangers' station. Says he'll be back Monday morning to pick you up. "What the hell are ya gonna do there for two frickin' days besides eat bugs, Mr. Hudson?"

"Fill a newspaper," you say with a laugh that isn't returned, now backing up the beach, wishing the other man would just leave before he catches sight of anything other than birds and bugs.

"I fill your newspapers with dead fish!" Sawyer grins, his shiny choppers glistening on the water. Animated now that you are separated by water, he puts his hands up like he's about to fend off your attack . . . and laughs so hard it looks like he might teeter and fall overboard.

You wave him off, still walking backwards to the dune and watching until the man stops being so pleased with himself. Then wait while the boat does a 180 and heads out to open water.

When you are certain that you won't be seen, you turn away from the old peeling Lifesaving Station and head across the dune and down a narrow sand path past the boarded-up Methodist Church and alongside a canal to what is known as O'Neal Cottage.

Someone had painted S. Lewis crudely on a scrap of washed-up wood nailed to the chipped-paint porch post.

The old place had seen better days. Much better days. Warped shakes on the roof. Paint flaking off the bared siding. Dry weathered posts. You think you might fall right through the badly rotted deck of the porch, but make it to the newly painted red screen door. When you finally knock on the wood, your heart is thudding so hard you have to turn around when you hear her voice coming from the darkness. "Peter, come in!"

You can't turn around. And you can barely get a sound out of your mouth, much less over the static in your ears. Staring through the glassy mist, you manage to say, "I actually don't think I can come in yet."

Talk about a flabby spirit. You know that your heart would seize at the very sight of her behind the screen. That if you didn't die from looking at her face, you would strangle her right there. Or worse, fall at her feet and beg her to come home with you.

She doesn't answer you, though. In fact, the silence goes on so long, you begin to think she's turned and left, maybe walked right out the back door.

But something butts the screen door open and there is something knocking the back of your legs. "Sit down, Peter, we can talk this way."

And so you, Peter Hudson, who have never liked to talk so much, sit in the wobbly chair and begin talking. And talking. And talking. You cry. You rail against everyone and everything you have ever known. And then you talk some more. The whole day, in fact.

Although you thought you were there to listen, when you start to speak you can't stop yourself, so many secrets and confidences that you can no longer hold inside, a boat pulled by the tides farther and farther out into the ocean.

So you tell her everything. Every shameful thing you did, everything Sarah told you or told Jessica who told you. Everything you had ever heard over the last four years. And everything you thought you had heard.

Mostly Brenda listens. Sometimes she lets out a sad little "Oh" or an "I'm so sorry." Sometimes just a muffled gasp or what sounds like fingernails scratching dry skin.

Early in the afternoon, during a long pause where you begin to panic that you've just run out of things to say—maybe fifteen or twenty minutes, your throat parched, you mind empty—Brenda slips a plate with five or six crabs onto the porch floor. They are covered with Old Bay. They are warm and your lips burn. A minute later there is a tall glass of sun-brewed iced tea—no ice.

After you devour the crabs, suck your fingers clean, toss the shells and gunk and the dead man's fingers out in front of the cottage for some crows who know that something is coming, you wipe your hands on your stained shorts and begin rehearsing inside your head the way you are going to tell her about Sarah and Buddy Neuse. You want her to feel exactly what you felt—what you still feel every time you look at Brendan.

So you talk and you talk and at some point begin to wonder if she has fallen asleep as you go on and on with the tape inside your head, just as you had gone on and on so often in your private grief. But after a chair scrapes the bare wooden floor she whispers, "I'm still listening, Peter." And you take some pleasure in knowing that every word stings like a jellyfish. And keeps stinging.

In the silences, you think you can hear a different scratching than fingernails along dry skin. No, this is her scratching something—a pen?—or maybe a pencil, a hand brushing away erasures? "Are you writing this down?" you suddenly accuse.

"Not really. I just don't want to forget anything, Peter. There's so much I don't know."

"Don't tell fucking anybody . . ." You can't finish, not sure what you are saying.

She cuts you off. "Now who would I tell? Everybody figures I'm dead."

"They're secrets, Brenda. No one will ever understand."

She doesn't respond.

Around dusk, the mosquitos sucking up big welts on your ankles, the crickets and peepers drowning out the buzzing in your brain, you think you hear the whir of a tape recorder, but Brenda just says "No" as if you're being ridiculous. You remember that tone.

That night you tell her, right before you curl up into the sleeping bag she tosses out on the porch, how Jessica came to you in the dunes and said she'd stay on Hatteras if you want her to. How she told you that Carson McCullers was right, but you didn't quite understand what she meant by that. How she also said you'd have to sell the cottage, and move to Salvo or Waves or anyplace away from Rodanthe and the pier.

And you tell her that you'll have Dana Covey list Caminada Bay as soon as you get back to Hatteras.

Brenda doesn't say a word.

* * *

But on the second day, when you finally grow weary of your own gravelly voice and tell her you're finished talking, Brenda actually begins her own reverie, her voice barely a whisper. She tells you first about her painting and her writing and growing vegetables and fishing, wasting time and breath until she finally meanders around to the whole long, involved story of her journey off the Outer Banks, all the way to New Orleans, her voice like the silky voice of a Jezebel behind you.

"All I can tell you, Peter, is that I was crazy. I was just thumb-suckin' insane, a mad woman . . . I must've been, you know, just blown away, driven from everything by the wind and the rain. I was so damn cold . . ." She pauses as if she sees someone approaching, but no one is there on the path. "But I remember every single moment of it as if it happened this morning. I just can't tell you why it happened or . . . how it went on so long. How I got so far away, but I did. You always read about men doing this, but not women, not a mom, not me."

You imagine the woman behind you shaking her head, reaching up solely out of habit to push the long straight hair away from her dark, wet eyes. It is hot; the back of your thighs stick to the vinyl chair. You can't breathe.

When she gets up and walks away, you're tempted, but don't turn. And when she comes back a minute or two later, you hear a match being struck and a deep breath drawn in, and a long thin line of smoke appears off to the side of your head.

She drops the pack of cigarettes and boxes of matches alongside the chair and says then that she remembers walking through the screen door onto the deck "that day," her whole body trembling, holding on to the rough two-by-six rail as she moved down the shaky steps to the sand, yelling from the road at Woody to get back in the cottage, then trudging over the dunes and up the beach toward the pier.

And she tells you how she knew, even back then, that she wasn't headed anyplace in particular, because there was nowhere to go; she was just walking the empty beach wondering how the hell her life had gotten so fenced in.

She remembers how the ocean was whipped up, waves surging up to the dunes, froth rolling across the barrier sands, then blowing in gusts south with the wind. Soon or not so soon she was all the way up on the northern stretch of National Seashore, breathing heavily, cheeks tingling both with fear and a kind of ecstasy that she had never before known.

Saying no finally to Rosslyn Hills felt like the most audacious few seconds she had ever known in her life.

"Perhaps even more audacious," she adds, "than saying 'I do' nineteen years ago to a man with whom I had not yet made love."

You wince at that.

"At first," she starts all over again, "all I wanted was to give you some time to settle down and really think about what I was talking about; what I had been talking about for years. Years. It was nothing new, the whole thing. I really couldn't take it anymore. If I was thinking at all, I thought I'd stay out on the beach for a few hours and worry you. I hoped—stupidly I guess—that you might agree to stay a few extra days and talk some more about it. But I really felt in my heart, that if I went back to Rosslyn I would die." You stare at a skimmer soaring toward the surf. "I couldn't go back there—and I honestly couldn't believe deep in my heart that you didn't agree with me; you always said you did, it was just that everything,

everything always got in the way.

"Peter, I still don't know how I got lost that day. I was miles away from the cottage when I realized how far I had gone. It was already around eleven when I reached the pier, then I ran down the beach to our path through the dunes.

"I got to the top of the dune expecting to see the blue van right where it had been, and Woody leaning on the rail of the deck searching the dunes, as if nothing had changed in the hours that I had been gone." She lets out an anguished moan. "I was waving as I took the final step over the dune and saw instantly that the driveway was empty; there was no one on the deck. The cottage all alone on an unneighborly strip of sand.

"My legs grew wobbly. I held tightly to the splintery rail up the steps and stumbled at the corroded handle on the screen door. It swung open with the wind, but the inner door was locked. I twisted the knob violently back and forth, back and forth.

"I was devastated. I probably would have stayed there all day, waiting for someone to find me and make you come back. But it started to rain. It was suddenly pouring, and so damn cold. And the two other cottages on the road were still shuttered up. I was alone on that empty strip of sand.

"I heard the storm door smashing back on the wall of the cottage and pushed myself up and walked right past it and didn't look back until I was halfway down the road."

Now you nod vacantly and light another cigarette off the burning end of the butt you have just smoked to the filter.

"I really didn't know what I was doing," she picks up after the cigarette pack and matches are back on the floor. "I didn't even know how I was standing up. It was like I was totally empty—no bones, no muscle, no heart, just a trembling bag of skin floating over the sandy potholes.

"And pretty soon after I was out on Highway 12, rain blowing across the sand in waffling sheets, I heard a car approaching from behind me, and the next thing I knew I was sticking out my thumb, thinking that I would just get a ride down to Salvo and figure it all out.

"It was a guy—a kid really—in one of those Ford Rancheros. He said he was going down to the ferry, and where was I going? and before I knew it I was shivering, the wet sweatshirt clinging to my skin, and thinking, *They must be at the Sand Dollar*, but when we got to Salvo, there was no van in front, and I just closed my eyes to stop the tears and within a minute or two the Sand Dollar was just a weepy memory in the big side-view mirror and everything went blank. When I woke up I was in New Orleans."

"Fuck you," you mumble out of the side of your mouth as the bright sun makes you squint.

* * *

A half hour later you break the noisy silence. "How do you live?" you say, finally.

"Simply." She laughs the laugh you remember. "Ve-ry simply."

"No, I mean, what do you do for money?"

"I write articles for dippy art and regional magazines." You suddenly recall the S. Lewis byline in the Cape Hatteras Electric's publication, *Carolina Country*, thinking it was a man and wondering if he'd like to write for the *Weekly*. "I think I've seen some of them," you mumble and reach for another cigarette.

"They're tripe, but they bring in a few dollars. I don't need much here. Just some cash for paints—and some paper and pencils—and stamps and rice. I grow some vegetables out back behind that wind fence." She stops talking then, and you imagine her bent over hills with cucumbers, tomatoes, and squash. "And I fish most days, crab on Saturdays. Mostly, I just get through each day. There's not much to say after that. And there's no one to talk to. I sing sometimes. I write a lot in my journal."

The blood runs from your head. "Don't you dare write about this, Brenda, not any of it."

When she doesn't answer, you suddenly feel too heavy for the rickety chair, as if the spindly legs are going to crack right through the rotting floor boards. If you could stand up right then, you would bolt off the deck. But as you can't move, you hold on tight to the sides of the wooden chair like you're on some kind of amusement-park ride.

And when you hear Sawyer's high-pitched yahooing from the beach, you feel her hand on your shoulder. "Come back sometime, Peter. Please. Sometime? There's still so much more to talk about."

"I don't know what," you say but can't manage to get up from the chair. "I don't think I could bear to see you—and that's the only reason to return."

"You haven't even looked."

"That's good for you, Brenda," you say. "I think I just want everything as I remember it."

"Please come back, Peter."

"I don't think so." And with that, you crank your head back, looking up at the porch ceiling's stained and rotting boards. "Don't you dare tell anybody. Anybody," you say over your shoulder.

"I promise. Please promise me to come back, Peter. Next April?"

You feel something on your shoulder, and a packet of papers, folded longwise, slides down your chest into your lap. "I wrote this about some of my time in New Orleans and then in Milwaukee. It might help you to understand."

You stand and slide the folded packet of paper into your back pocket, and when Sawyer bellows into the wind again, you stand and walk down off the porch. Pull the pages from your pocket. Tear them in half. And then, struggling, tearing them in half again, and half again, toss them up in the wind.

Epilogue

As it turns out, though, you can't stay away. Once a year you return. And you eventually hear the whole story. It's not a new story. Old as the wind and the tides.

And as you now probably realize, Brenda's promises weren't worth her salt.

###